Outta Sight

• Mary Blakeslee •

Cover by Brian Boyd

Scholastic-TAB Publications Ltd.

Scholastic-TAB Publications Ltd.
123 Newkirk Road, Richmond Hill, Ontario, Canada L4C 3G5

Scholastic Inc.
730 Broadway, New York, NY 10003, USA

Ashton Scholastic Pty Limited
PO Box 579, Gosford, NSW 2250, Australia

Ashton Scholastic Limited
165 Marua Road, Panmure, Auckland 6, New Zealand

Scholastic Publications Ltd.
10 Earlham Street, London, WC2H 9LN, UK

Canadian Cataloguing in Publication Data

Blakeslee, Mary
   Outta Sight

ISBN 0-590-71376-0

I. Title.

PS8553.L34088 1987   jC813'.54   C87-094253-0

PZ7.B58Ou 1987

6 5 4 3 2 1   Printed in Canada   7 8 9/8

Manufactured by Webcom Limited

To Claire Branner
For all her help and encouragement

Contents

Chapter 1
If only something would happen

"Hold it! Great! Now turn — smile. That's it. Throw your head back and let your hair fan out. Sensational! Now another big smile. Beautiful! There, that should wrap it up. Another perfect session. Hope, you're the best I've ever worked with."

The little man with the camera gave me a thumbs up salute and began to pack up his equipment. I threw on a mink jacket over my designer swimsuit and walked languorously to my dressing room. I opened the door and saw that the usual mass of red roses was sitting on the dressing table. No note, of course. I wondered who my secret admirer was. Could it be that Count I had met at Nice last year? Or maybe the star of . . .

* * *

"Hope, come on, wake up! Shirley and I are both ready to go and you still haven't got your bathing suit on."

I snapped back to reality, leaving my secret admirer behind along with my dazzling career as a high-priced fashion model, and entered the dull world of Kamloops, British Columbia, Wednesday, June 28th, 1944.

"I'm sorry, Anna," I apologized, jumping up and reaching for my red and white satin suit with the skirt that I pretended hid my bulging hips and stomach. "I'll just be a minute. I was thinking about my career," I grinned.

"Yeah, you start at McNeil's on Monday, don't you?" Shirley asked. "It should be fun being a soda jerk." She licked her lips. "Just think of all those free sundaes and milk shakes."

Shirley is almost twenty pounds heavier than me and a couple of inches shorter, which, I'm afraid, makes her look a little like a female Lou Costello. Anna, on the other hand, weighs about ninety pounds soaking wet and has the perfect figure that so many Japanese Canadian girls are blessed with.

"Sure it'll be great," I answered Shirley, "but I hate to think what it'll do to my complexion. I have so many spots now that I look like I'm suffering from a raging case of smallpox."

"They don't show too much," Anna assured me as we stuffed our clothes in our lockers. "Your bangs cover most of your forehead and the sides hide your cheeks."

I laughed and put my arm around her shoulder. "Thanks, Anna, but I know what I look like, and I don't really care. Beauty is only skin-deep and all that stuff."

But I did care; I cared a lot.

It wasn't that I didn't have boyfriends — I probably had more last year than any other girl in grade nine. But that's exactly what they were — friends. I went to all the parties, sure, but I spent most of the time in the kitchen on voluntary KP. Better a scullery maid than a wallflower, I figured. I had never had a real date in my entire life. Last year I was Junior High president and head of the grad dance committee — and I went to the dance with Shirley. Fat and pimply just don't make you prom queen. I was hoping that next fall when I'd be in senior high things would change. But I wasn't taking any bets.

We left the change room and started across the grass to the river. On the way we had to pass the lifeguard's tower where the most gorgeous male-type person in the entire northwest sits from ten to six every day making sure that no one gets carried away by the current. Johnny La Longa is a friend of my brother, Jeff, although he's a year older.

"Hey, Hope," he called down as we came closer, "tell Jeff I got my letter today. They accepted me in the Air Force. I leave for camp next week."

I grinned up at him and said, "That's great, Johnny. Jeff'll be green though. He still has to wait till next spring."

So someone I knew was actually getting into the war. It had been going on for nearly five years, but you'd never know it by living in Kamloops. Sure a lot of the older guys had joined up, but they weren't anyone I had much to do with. There was neither a military camp nor a factory anywhere near the city, so everyone who was involved with doing their bit for the war effort left town. The closest most of us came to suffering was sugar and gas rationing and knitting khaki mittens.

Shirley and Anna had gone ahead and I ran to catch up. But I was terribly conscious of Johnny's eyes following my dumpy figure as I reached

4

the edge of the river and waded in. I must have looked like a sea turtle heading back to the ocean after laying her eggs.

We swam out to the raft and lay on our stomachs to dry off. My glasses, which I had to wear constantly if I wanted to see large buildings, were spotted with water, and my bathing cap had a rip up one side.

"I guess you guys saw how Johnny watched me," I kidded. "I think he's secretly in love with me."

"Oh, Hope, you're such a clown," Anna laughed. "Aren't you ever serious?"

It was pretty ridiculous, all right: Johnny La Longa looking at me twice. I tried to laugh along with Anna, but it didn't come off too well. I could feel depression settling in and knew I needed a chocolate fix.

"I think I'll swim back and get something to eat," I announced, standing up and stuffing my hair back under my cap.

"We just got here, Hope," Anna protested. "Don't you —"

"I'm right behind you," Shirley rolled over and sat up. "I could use a little something myself."

I watched her struggle to her feet, her body

straining against the black wool of her too small suit, and felt a little guilty about encouraging her. But right now I was too busy feeling sorry for myself to really worry about anyone else.

The hot fudge sundae did a lot to revive my spirits, at least temporarily. A bunch of the kids from our class were in the soda fountain attached to the pavilion, and they all squeezed together in the booth to make room for us. I've got to tell you, it took a lot of squeezing.

"Did you hear about Johnny?" someone asked.

"Yeah," I replied. "He sure is lucky." My mind began to replay all the great war movies I'd seen in the last couple of years. I would have given anything to join up myself, but the government was pretty clear about not taking fat fifteen-year-olds in the WACs. So instead of mopping wounded men's foreheads and driving jeeps through London during an air raid, I'd be jerking sodas at McNeil's and studying French with M. Lasseur. Life just wasn't fair.

"Dear God," I pleaded silently, "please make something exciting happen to me before I'm too old to enjoy it."

When we finished our sundaes, we went to the counter to pay our bill. With the dime I still had left, I bought two Baby Ruth chocolate bars to keep me going till dinner. Anna and Shirley wanted to swim back to the wharf, but I decided not to go with them. I had a new movie magazine waiting for me in my room and a new Sinatra record on my portable record player. So I went into the locker room, changed back to my sloppy joe and jeans, and walked the ten blocks up the hill to my house.

When I opened the door, I knew immediately that something was wrong. Dad was home and it was only three in the afternoon. I could hear him and Mom talking in the kitchen, and it sounded like Mom was crying. I threw my wet suit and towel on the hall floor and ran to the kitchen door.

"What's the matter?" I cried.

Mom looked up from the table where she and Dad were sitting over cups of coffee. Her eyes were red and she was twisting a soiled hanky between her fingers.

"Oh, Hope, it's your cousin, Brian. Aunt Rose phoned an hour or so ago. He's been listed as missing in action."

I slipped slowly into a chair and stared at her. Oh, God, I thought, when I asked you to make something exciting happen, I sure didn't mean this.

* * *

Our family is very close. We have to be, there are so few of us. Mom is an only child and Dad has one sister, Aunt Rose. She and Uncle Arnie have two children: Brian who is nineteen and Lila who is two years younger. And that's it. I haven't seen my cousins since two Christmases ago when we went to visit them in Vancouver. But, as I said, we're very close and anything that affects them affects us too.

"Oh, poor Aunt Rose — she must be really scared," I said at last. Then I remembered Lila and how she adored Brian. "And Lila, how is she taking it? Do you know?"

Mom sniffed again and blew her nose before answering. Her voice when she spoke was low and sad.

"Lila is devastated. Rose doesn't know what to do about her."

I could understand that. Lila didn't have a lot going for her, and to lose Brian would be enough to send her crashing. I'm fat and not great looking, but Lila is, if possible, worse. She's tall and blonde and weighs about 175 pounds.

She slumps and her hair is stringy and she has worse acne than me. Do you get the picture? I wished I was in Vancouver so I could at least give her a little cousinly support.

But did I need to be in Vancouver? Why couldn't Lila come here? It would be a bit of a drag having her around all summer — it certainly wouldn't do a thing for my popularity rating; she could scare more boys away than the Bride of Frankenstein — but that was beside the point. She was my cousin and she needed help.

"Mom, why don't you see if Lila would like to come up here for the summer? It would get her away from all the things that remind her of Brian. She could sleep in my room — I sure don't need both twin beds."

Mom and Dad looked at each other, and Dad nodded.

"That's an excellent idea," Mom agreed. "I'll call tonight and see how she feels about it. You're sure you don't mind? I know you have your own friends, and an older cousin could be a nuisance."

"Absolutely not, she won't be any trouble. From what I can remember, she spends most of her time reading books, listening to the radio and making candy."

"Yes, poor little thing. Maybe I'll call right

now." She got up from the table and went out into the hall.

"Does Jeff know about Brian?" I asked Dad.

"Not yet. I'm almost afraid to tell him," Dad admitted. "He's always looked up to Brian as a sort of idol. God knows how this news will affect him."

I remembered Johnny's news about joining the R.C.A.F. and realized that Dad did have a lot to worry about. Jeff was pretty impulsive. I wouldn't put it past him to run away, lie about his age, and join up himself. I needed to talk to him before he did something stupid. I got up from the table and went over to where Dad sat slumped in his chair. I put my hand on his shoulder.

"Would you like me to tell him, Dad? Sometimes it's easier to hear stuff like this from someone your own age."

"That's good of you, Hope. Maybe you're right."

I gave him the V-for-Victory sign and went out the back door.

Jeff works as a mechanic's helper at McCallum's garage after school and weekends and full-time during the summer. He's a super brother and I love everything about him except one thing:

his looks. He got Dad's blond hair and perfect face and body, whereas I inherited Mom's dark hair, fat cells and near-sightedness. It wasn't fair. The funny thing is, I don't think he even knows he's so good-looking. He has every girl over twelve with normal glands drooling over him, but he doesn't date more than once or twice a month. I guess he just hasn't met the right girl yet.

I found him halfway under the hood of a 1928 Ford. The car had definitely seen better days, but anything that still had a motor and tires was being resurrected. Car manufacturers had stopped production back in '41 when the Americans came into the war, and the shortage of operating autos was drastic.

He raised his head and looked over his shoulder when I called to him from the doorway to the office.

"Oh, hi, Hopeless. What are you doing down here?"

"Can you stop for a drink? I've got something to tell you."

"Sure. Just wait till I wash some of this grease off my hands and I'll be right with you."

He went into the men's, and I got two Orange Crushes from the cooler. When he came in, I gave him one of the bottles and sat down. There was no way to soften the blow, so I gave it to him straight.

"It's about Brian, Jeff. He's missing in action. Aunt Rose just phoned."

He didn't say anything for a few minutes. He just sat there staring at the bubbles in the pop bottle. Finally he took a big gulp of orange and spoke.

"That does it. I'm not staying around here any longer. I'm going to Vancouver and enlist."

"No, Jeff. That's just dumb. In a few months you'll be eighteen and you can do it properly — get into the Air Force like Johnny. This way you'll just be a buck private sloshing around in the mud someplace with an unpronounceable name."

"Johnny in the Air Force? What are you talking about?"

"I saw him at the park today. He asked me to tell you he got his letter."

He threw the half full bottle across the room and swore. I watched the orange foam run down the wall and didn't speak.

"Thanks for telling me, Hope," he said at last. "I've got to get back to that little Ford. The guy's coming in at five to pick it up."

"You won't do anything without telling me, will you, Jeff?"

He patted my shoulder as he passed me. "Maybe not. I just don't know." He walked out of the room and over to the black coupe.

I knew I should go home and tell Mom and Dad what Jeff had threatened to do. They could legally stop him, I was sure. But I didn't. He had to make his own decision, and I had to let him. Instead, I walked the four blocks to Anna's parents' dry cleaning shop.

Anna was still at the park, but her sister Marie was behind the desk. Marie is Jeff's age, and even more gorgeous than Anna. I often thought she and Jeff would make a great couple, but whenever I mentioned it to people, they'd get this stunned look on their faces and blurt out, "But she's Japanese!" like it was some form of the plague.

"Anna's not here, Hope," Marie said as I came through the door. "I thought she'd be with you. Do you know where she is?"

"At the park with Shirley. I left them an hour or so ago. I was hoping she'd be home by now; I need to talk to her."

"So do we," Marie answered. "We need her help. I guess I'll have to go find her."

"Why? What's up?"

"Mom's brother and his family are coming here tonight. We have to clean out Anna's room and get it ready for the kids. They'll be staying with us until they can find a place of their own."

"Why are they coming here? I thought your uncle had a big business in Vancouver?"

"Where were you when the war began, Hope? That was years ago." Marie's tone was bitter. "Don't you know that back in '42 all the 'dirty little traitorous Japs' living on the coast were relocated to the interior where they couldn't send war secrets back to Japan? My uncle and his family have been living in New Denver in practically a concentration camp for the past two years."

"Come on, Marie. You can't mean your family! Anna told me you've lived in Canada for three generations. You're more Canadian than I am, for gosh sakes."

"Tell it to the War Department."

"But that's totally unfair! Haven't you got a cousin in the American army?"

"Sure. He's in the 442nd fighting in Italy, but that doesn't seem to make any difference. Two years ago my uncle was forced to sell his business for what he could get and the family was sent to the interior with nothing but what they could carry with them. Everything they owned — their furniture, car, boat — all had to be left behind. Eventually the government sold off their stuff and everyone else's by auction, but my uncle sure didn't get much for it.

"Dad just recently managed to get permission to bring them here. I guess the B.C. politicians who've been wanting to get rid of the Japanese for years couldn't come up with a good enough reason why my uncle would be trying to engage in any fifth column activities here in isolated Kamloops."

"You mean our government really did things like that to people? That's hard to believe."

"Believe it. My family didn't even have it as bad as some. The people who weren't as well-off as my uncle were forced into living in livestock stalls in Vancouver before they were evacuated."

How could all this have been happening without me knowing a thing about it? Maybe, I thought with a pang of guilt, it was because the only thing I read in the papers was Orphan Annie.

"We're going to have a house guest too," I told Marie, shrugging off the uncomfortable feeling and trying to change the subject. "My cousin's coming here for the summer — at least I think she is. Her brother's just been reported missing in action."

"Oh, I'm so sorry, Hope. Here I am complaining about our family having to leave their home and you've . . . " Her face started to crumple.

"Yeah, I know. Let's just forget it. Hey look, maybe we can all get together soon. You can bring your cousins over to our house to meet us, and Lila can meet you. Sound good?"

"Sure, that would be great," she smiled. "Thanks, Hope. I know they'll really appreciate the gesture."

"Good. I'll talk to Anna and set it up with Mom. Sometime next week, eh?"

She nodded and I turned to leave just as the door opened and a tall, sandy-haired creature came into the shop. I stood there and stared as he walked past me to the counter.

"I need these by tomorrow if possible," he said as Marie began to sort out the pants and jackets he dropped in front of her. "I'll be in to pick them up at five-thirty."

"No trouble," she answered and handed him a claim slip. He took it and turned to walk back to the door. I was still standing on the threshold gaping like a retarded trout. He paused, waiting for me to get out of his way so he could leave.

"Coming or going?" he finally asked when I showed no sign of moving.

Slowly the gears began to grind again and I jumped aside.

"Going. Coming. Going," I answered smartly.

He hesitated, gave me a strange look, then shook his head and went out the door.

"Who was that?" I managed to sputter.

"Troy Farnham, old Mrs. Ellis's nephew," Marie answered. "He just came into town a week or so ago. He's staying with her for the summer, so I hear."

"Did you see him? He looks just like Van Johnson, only better." I went to the door and opened it in a kind of daze. I guess I said goodbye to Marie; I don't remember.

Walking slowly home, I thought of all the things that had happened so far today. June 28th would stay with me a long time. I would always remember it as the day my cousin was reported missing, the day I learned about the evacuation of Canadian citizens from their homes, the day Johnny joined up. And the day that I met the star of all my fantasies in the flesh.

Chapter 2
Lila arrives

Dad had gone back to work when I got home. Mom was sitting in the living room with all the blinds pulled and wet towels on her legs, arms and head. A portable fan was stirring hot air in front of her face. She looked about as bad as I felt.

"Did you get hold of Aunt Rose?" I yelled above the noise of the fan as I came into the room.

She removed the towel from her head and turned the fan off.

"Yes, I did. Lila is taking the train tomorrow night; she'll be here Friday morning. Did you talk to Jeff?"

"That's great," I cried, ignoring her question and starting back out of the room. "I'll run upstairs right now and make up the other bed. She'll need drawer and closet space too, so I'd better — "

"It's all done, Hope. Now what about Jeff?"

I turned back and slumped into a chair.

"I told him. He was pretty upset. Johnny La Longa enlisted in the Air Force and is leaving for camp next week. I guess Jeff feels he'd like to get more involved."

"That's nonsense. He's only seventeen. Besides, he spends three nights a week at Air Cadets and sells Victory Bonds. I don't know what more he could do."

I wasn't about to tell her, so I changed the subject.

"I saw Marie Suzuki too, and she told me her family is expecting relatives from Vancouver tonight. Well, from New Denver actually, but they used to live in Vancouver. She said they were forced to leave their home and business there a couple of years ago — they were a security risk or something."

Mom sighed. "This crazy war, it's making people do horrible, ridiculous things. Mrs. Ganz told me this morning when I was shopping that a bunch of hoodlums broke into their store last night and pulled everything off the shelves. Then they wrote 'Dirty Nazis' in soap on all the windows."

"But they've been in Kamloops forever," I protested. "I don't think they've ever even been to Germany."

"That doesn't seem to matter to our 'patriotic' citizens."

I shook my head and stood up.

"I'm going up to my room to read for awhile. Call me if you want help with dinner."

She didn't answer. The towel was back in place and the fan was on again. I figured she wanted to be alone too.

When I got to my room, I picked up the movie magazine from the desk, put my new Sinatra record on the turntable, and flopped down on the bed. I opened the magazine to the middle where a full-page close-up of Van Johnson smiled out at me. He looked exactly like Troy Farnham, only older. I lay there and stared at it, while from the record player Frankie was whispering about how half a love never appealed to him. I put aside the magazine, rolled onto my stomach and closed my eyes.

*   *   *

"I've been watching you from across the room ever since you came in, and I can't stand it any longer. I have to meet you."

I turned around in surprise and there, leaning over the couch, was Troy Farnham. I smiled up at him and adjusted the strap on my pink formal.

"Won't you sit down?" I patted the seat beside me.

"You're the most beautiful girl at this dance," he whispered, dropping down next to me. "But I can't understand why you're not dancing. Every man here has eyes only for you."

"I guess I've been waiting for the right partner," I answered with a slight blush.

He reached over and put his hand over mine.

"And might I just possibly qualify?"

"Possibly." I stood up. "Shall we see?"

He took me into his arms and we moved onto the dance floor. The music surrounded us like a warm cloud. I closed my eyes and rested my head on his broad shoulder.

*   *   *

"Hope, you're going to ruin that record if you don't lift the needle," Mom called outside my door. "It's been going around in the middle for at least five minutes."

I jumped up and lifted the arm off the record. The needle was as blunt as a nail. I changed it, turned the record over and sat down at the dressing table. The face staring at me from the oval mirror would never turn Troy Farnham on in a million years. Black bangs down to my steel-rimmed glasses, skin that looked like red tapioca — I was a winner, all right. I smeared on some vanishing cream from the new jar I had picked up at Woolworth's the day before. If it would do only half what the ad promised, I'd look like a Woodbury deb in a week. But I knew it wouldn't.

Discouraged, I picked up the magazine from the floor and, remembering the Baby Ruths I had bought earlier, reached for my beach bag.

When Mom called me for dinner a while later I wasn't hungry, but I knew I had to make an appearance or everyone would worry. So I got up, washed the glop off my face, combed my hair and went downstairs.

Everyone was at the table when I came into the dining room. Mom and Dad were still wearing their doomsday faces, and Jeff looked angry enough to bite the table leg. I decided someone had to try to cheer things up, so I sat down in my chair and made myself smile.

"Did you guys hear about the little moron who ran back and forth on the cereal box because it said 'Tear Around the Top'?"

"Groan," said Jeff.

Mom started to smile in spite of herself and looked over at Dad.

"I guess there's no point in going into mourning, is there?" she said. "Brian will turn up — he's a survivor. And Lila doesn't need a bunch of zombies to spend the summer with."

"Lila's coming here! When? Why?" Jeff no longer looked angry; he looked terrified.

"She'll be in Friday morning. And as to why she's coming, I think you can probably figure that out for yourself, Jeff." Mom gave him a dirty look and started passing the vegetables.

"Oh, God! Will she expect me to take her out, do you think? Now don't get me wrong, I like Lila just fine, but she's so ... so ... "

"I wouldn't worry, Jeff," I answered. "She'll probably just want to sit around and listen to 'Ma Perkins' and 'Pepper Young's Family.' That and read. It's all she did when we were in Vancouver."

"Yeah, that's right." He sounded relieved.

"Maybe we could have some people in to meet her," Mom offered.

That reminded me about Anna's relatives and my offer to Marie. I told Dad and Jeff the story of their being relocated and finally getting permission to come to Kamloops, and how they would be arriving about the same time as Lila.

"So I suggested to Marie that we have a party here at the house so everyone could meet everyone else," I finished. "Good idea?"

"Good enough, as long as you have it on a night I have to be at Cadets."

"Come on, Jeff, it won't kill you to be charming for just one night. Besides, Marie will be there."

"Look, Hope, it won't do you any good to promote. I'm not interested in Marie Suzuki."

"How about next Saturday?" Mom asked. "It's about the only night everyone is free."

"Great," I said. "I'll ask Shirley and a couple of other kids, and you can ask some of your friends, Jeff. Maybe someone who's new in town and doesn't know anybody yet."

Jeff gave me a funny look and said, "Like who?"

"Oh, I don't know. I just thought there might be somebody visiting from out of town."

"You've seen Troy Farnham, I gather. Well, don't get your hopes up. Every girl in town has her eye on him."

I could feel the blush start at my neck and shoot up to my hairline.

"I didn't mean anyone in particular," I protested. Everyone looked knowingly at me, and I knocked over my iced tea. "I think I'd better phone Anna right now." I jumped up from the table and ran upstairs to the hall phone before Mom could call me back to eat my green beans and beets. I hate living in a family of know-it-all mind readers.

*　　*　　*

I was asleep when Lila actually arrived on Friday. The train gets in at some unholy hour like four A.M., so only Dad went to the station to meet her. When I woke up, she was asleep in the bed next to me. At least, I assumed the lump under the blanket was Lila — all I could see of her was a strand of blonde hair.

I got up, threw on my clothes without waking her and went down to see about breakfast. No one was in sight. As I poured myself a glass of chocolate milk, I decided everyone had probably stayed up till all hours talking and were sleeping in. I had gone to bed early with the idea of waking when she arrived, but I obviously slept through the whole thing.

A glance showed me it was only six-thirty. No wonder I seemed to be the only person conscious in the universe. That's what you get for folding at nine o'clock. I was far too wide awake to go back to bed, so I grabbed a handful of cookies and went out onto the back porch.

It was a sparkling morning — cool and fresh. The only sounds were the chirping of a robin as he hopped around looking for a late worm, and the gentle whir of a sprinkler down the street. I sat down on the step, bit into a cookie and let my mind plan the day.

I would take Lila down to the park if she wanted to go, and let her meet some of my friends. On second thought, maybe that wasn't such a good idea. One blimp in a bathing suit was bad enough; two would be positively terrifying. Maybe we could just sit around the house and get to know one another again. Probably she would want to listen to the soap operas on the radio. That would kill quite a bit of time. She could meet my friends at the party next week.

The party, of course, whipped my mind directly to Troy Farnham, and I started another of my fantasies. I was just getting to the part where he was pulling me out of the river and begging me not to die, when I heard the door open.

"Hi," a voice purred behind me. "Mind if I join you?"

I jerked around and found myself staring at a pair of legs that would make Betty Grable weak with envy. My glance travelled upward. A blonde goddess was standing there, holding a glass of orange juice and smiling at me.

"Lila?" I croaked. "Is that you?"

"You were expecting maybe Groucho Marx?" she laughed.

"Yes. No. Well, not exactly. Here, sit down." I gestured to the step and proceeded to choke on my cookie.

"Hey, are you okay?" Lila bent down and patted me on the back. "I didn't mean to startle you."

"That's all right," I managed after a moment or two of spewing cookie crumbs all over the porch. "It was just such a shock to see you . . . up so soon," I finished lamely.

She sat down beside me and took a sip of juice.

I continued to stare at her in total amazement. How could that weird-looking girl I remembered possibly be this incredible creature sitting beside me? Maybe there was something to that fairy godmother stuff after all. I suddenly realized that her mouth was moving. She must be talking to me.

"Oh, I'm usually an early riser," she was saying. "I try to exercise for half an hour or so before breakfast when I'm home. Brian got me into the habit." Her smile faded and her face got a kind of strained look. I bit into my cookie and turned away, embarrassed both for her and for myself. I felt like I had walked into someone's bad dream and couldn't find my way out.

"Uh, it's going to be another hot one, I guess," I reported. Nothing like the weather to make for scintillating conversation.

She didn't answer. I finally got up courage to look at her again and nearly died. She was crying. Holy Toledo! What was I supposed to do? I couldn't just sit there. She looked so unhappy and kind of lost. Gradually, as I watched her, my embarrassment disappeared and I moved over and put my arm around her. She buried her head in my shoulder and sobbed.

"Go ahead and cry, Lila," I said. "I understand."

"I'm so scared for Brian," she whispered between sobs. "If he's really dead, I don't think I want to go on living either."

I patted her on the shoulder and muttered, "I sort of know how you must be feeling. I'd be out of my mind if it were Jeff."

I had said that just to comfort her, but I suddenly realized that it could well *be* Jeff. I knew he was thinking very seriously of running off to enlist, and I wouldn't be able to stop him if he did decide to. My heart started to flipflop, but when Lila sniffed a couple of times and drew away from me, I turned my attention back to her.

"It's going to be so great being here with you all summer, Hope. It'll be like having a sister — someone to talk to who'll understand."

"Yeah," I grinned slowly, "it will be, won't it?"

I was beginning to realize that it would be great to have her around. I'd always wanted an older sister, someone I could ask about stuff and get advice from. And besides, it sure wouldn't do my social life any harm to be seen with someone as beautiful as her.

"I was sort of afraid to come," she said. "Afraid you wouldn't want me around. It can be a drag feeling you have to entertain a relative. I promise, though, I won't interfere with any of your plans."

I thought of my recently made plans and started to laugh. Scratch "Ma Perkins" and "Pepper Young's Family."

"The only plans I have are to start work on

Monday at McNeil's Soda Fountain and to study French. French in the morning, McNeil's at noon and in the evening. We'll still have the afternoons together. We can go swimming a lot if you like."

"That sounds super. Swimming's my favourite sport. I even have my senior swimming and lifesaving certificates. I got them last year while I was trying to lose weight."

I cleared my throat and said, "Speaking of losing weight, you sure have changed since I saw you a couple of years ago."

She broke into a laugh that positively tinkled.

"Wasn't I revolting? Mom and Dad were about ready to send me to a convent by the time something happened and I finally decided to do something about myself."

"What happened?" I held my breath, expecting her to reveal the secret of eternal beauty.

"I fell in love," she grinned. "He didn't know I was alive, of course, so I decided I'd have to rely on something more than my terrific backstroke and my spoon collection to get him interested. So I did something about my looks."

"And did he notice you?" I was beginning to

see a parallel here that might just have some potential.

"Oh, sure. But when I got to know him, I found out he was a jerk. Still, he did give me the motivation to smarten up about myself."

She stood up and reached down for my hand.

"Okay, let's you give me a tour of your town now before breakfast. I intend to have a terrific summer here, and so will you. No more gloom and doom allowed. Brian is still alive — I'm sure of it. If he were dead, I'd know."

I stood up and nodded. She sure was being strong, when I knew how worried she was inside. "Okay," I answered in the same tone, "we'll start with beautiful downtown Kamloops, such as it is."

And as we walked side by side up toward Victoria Street, I couldn't help thinking that maybe this *would* be a terrific summer at that.

When we got back to the house an hour later, the rest of the family was up and having breakfast. Mom and Dad looked over as we came in the back door and smiled.

"You're up early, Lila," Mom remarked. "I thought you would sleep in after your late night."

"Too much excitement, I guess. Besides, it

gave Hope and me a chance to get to know one another again."

She sat down and beamed at everyone.

Jeff, who is not one of your morning people, was sitting in his rumpled pyjamas, hair standing straight up, pouring milk on a bowl of cereal. He was watching the stream coming from the pitcher and yawning.

"You might try waking up enough to say hello to your cousin, Jeff," Dad chided him. "After all, you haven't seen her for over two years."

Jeff raised lazy eyes, then did a double-take. The milk poured over the edge of the bowl and onto the table as he sat there staring like a moron.

"Jeff, the milk!" Mom's voice was anger tinged with amusement.

Jeff came out of his daze and stumbled to his feet.

"I — I'm sorry. I'll mop it up." He rushed to the sink and tripped on the cat.

Somehow he got the milk cleaned up without once taking his eyes off Lila. A gnawing little doubt started to creep over me. He couldn't take his eyes off Lila and he was her cousin. Ergo, no other male with normal glands would be able to see anyone but her either. When I was with her,

I'd be even more unnoticeable. And if anyone did notice me, I wouldn't exactly benefit by the comparison. "Pepper Young's Family" and long talks in the backyard started to look pretty good again.

While I was pondering this problem, Lila and Jeff started talking.

"I'm afraid I'm tied up all day," he began like some big shot movie producer, "but I'm free tonight. I'd be glad to show you around — introduce you to some of my friends."

"Thanks, Jeff, but I think I'll go to bed early. I didn't get much sleep last night."

"Tomorrow then. One of the guys is having a wiener roast out on his farm. Would you like to go?"

"Sure, that would be fun, but you must have a date already."

"No, no," Jeff hastened to assure her. "It's just a bunch of kids getting together — not couples."

"Okay, then." She turned to me. "What are you wearing, Hope?"

"But she's not — " He stopped. Mom had obviously got his shin pretty good under the table. He winced and shut up. As for me, I didn't know whether to burst out in wild song or throw myself on the nearest garbage truck. I had never been out with Jeff's crowd, and it was more than even my vivid imagination could handle.

I guess Mom must have noticed the weird looks on both our faces and decided it was time to change the subject.

"What are your plans for the day, Hope?"

"Well, I told Shirley and Anna I'd meet them at the park at ten, but since Lila's awake, I think I'll cancel."

"No, don't do that on account of me. I'm going to spend the day getting my clothes and stuff straightened out and writing some letters. You go ahead with your plans and I'll see you tonight."

I decided to take her up on the offer. It would be the last time that Shirley, Anna and I would be able to spend a lazy afternoon together at the park when it was quiet. We were all starting work on Monday and would be free together only on weekends when the park was packed with people. Besides, I needed to be with old friends so I wouldn't have to think for awhile. Things were moving just too darned fast, and I wasn't sure I could keep up.

Chapter 3
Drastic measures

We were upstairs in my room getting dressed for the wiener roast. I had decided at least ten times in the past twenty-four hours not to go, but Lila insisted. So here I was, stuffing my way into a pair of jeans that used to fit me twenty pounds ago and wondering if it would be dark enough at the farm to hide the three new pimples that had volunteered on my chin overnight.

Lila was poured into white seersucker slacks and a halter top that showed off her perfect back. Her skin was as smooth as a two-year-old's. We looked very interesting together — like a before and after ad in the back of *True Romances*.

Lila was watching me as I combed my hair over my eyebrows and tried to make it cover my chin.

"You have lovely hair, Hope," she remarked, "but aren't those bangs kind of hot?"

"Well, sort of," I admitted, "but I have this skin condition . . . "

She smiled ruefully and said, "I know. I used to try to hide my awful skin too. I thought if I smeared on enough pancake make-up it wouldn't show. Of course, I was just kidding myself. It wasn't until some kid asked me what mime troupe I was with that I decided I'd better smarten up."

I looked at her perfect complexion and asked the question I'd been dying to ask since she appeared on the back porch the morning before.

"So what did you do to get skin like you've got now? It looks better than the three-year-old's I baby-sit."

"I found that my diet was the cause of most of my skin problems — that and my oily hair. When I cut out the candy bars and washed my hair every day, my skin cleared up."

Washing my hair every day I could handle, although I was a little concerned that it would dissolve from too much shampoo. But give up sweets? I didn't think that was possible. Candy and malts and chocolate layer cake were the only things that made life bearable. Whenever the world seemed to be tilting on me, I could always straighten it with a shot of sugar.

I was saved from having to make any comment by Jeff yelling up at us to hurry. He still wasn't crazy about having to drag his little sister to the party where I know he was planning a big entrance with Lila. He hadn't said anything, but the signs were there.

I quickly threw on a big plaid shirt that covered me almost to my knees and reached for the pancake make-up. Lila was already on her way downstairs, so I gave myself one last coating of paint and ran after her. So I looked like a clown — better that than looking like a strawberry custard.

Jeff's little coupe held two people in the front seat quite comfortably. Three was like squeezing a Sherman tank into an elevator. Jeff's solution was for me to sit by myself in the rumble seat, but Lila wouldn't hear of it.

"I'll sit back here with you," she said, climbing in beside me. "Rumble seats are fun — much better than being cooped up inside."

Jeff started to protest, then, realizing it wouldn't do a bit of good, shrugged his shoulders and started the motor.

I was beginning to realize there was more to Lila than just a pretty, reconditioned face.

The Rounds farm was in North Kamloops

about five miles from town. The property went down to the North Thompson River, and as we drove up to the house we could see a huge bonfire burning on the sandbank. Jeff parked the car in the driveway and came around to the back to help us climb out. He practically lifted Lila bodily from the seat and set her on the ground like she was a piece of rare crystal. I scrambled out by myself, and as he escorted her down to the fire, pulled out blankets and food. I was sorely tempted to crawl back into the rumble seat and sleep until the party was over. No one would notice I was missing, I was sure. But while I was standing there thinking about it, someone came out of the darkness calling my name.

"Hey, Hope, let me give you a hand with that stuff."

I turned around and saw Raymond Rounds loping toward the car.

Raymond is Jeff's age and one of his best pals, although I'll never know why. Raymond is your typical brain who doesn't go in much for sports, whereas Jeff is a straight C student and captain of the basketball team. Ray's not bad looking if you like redheads with freckles, but there's one thing kind of creepy about him. He's got one finger missing from his left hand. Jeff told me he lost it playing hockey when he was just a kid and that's why he's not into athletics. He's been to the house hundreds of times and has always been very polite to me, but he'd sure never shown any interest before. I figured Jeff had sent him on the rescue mission.

"Thanks, Ray," I said, handing him a load of blankets and reaching back into the car for the pop. "I guess Jeff must have told you I was stuck with this stuff, eh?"

"No, it was your cousin. She was going to come back here herself when she saw you weren't with them, but I offered to go instead."

Ray took my arm as we worked our way through the silent blackness to the river where sixteen or so kids were sitting around a huge fire toasting marshmallows. Jeff and Lila were still standing as we came forward. Jeff had apparently been introducing Lila to the crowd, and Ray and I were just in time to see the reaction. The guys all looked like they wished they could comb their hair, and the girls looked like they would be awfully happy if Lila fell headfirst into the river. Lila was smiling at everyone.

I scanned the crowd as best I could in the dim firelight and realized I was the only one there who wasn't a senior. Not that it mattered; no one even noticed I'd arrived. They were all staring at Lila.

When we finally got seated around the fire and Ray went to put the pop on ice, Lila began to talk — not to the guys but to the girls. She was so friendly and warm that she had them completely won over in about five minutes. Meanwhile the guys continued to preen, trying to get her attention, but she was politely distant.

Then we heard a car drive up near the house and stop. A few minutes later Johnny La Longa, God's gift to lifeguarding, came into the glow of the fire. He and Lila saw each other about the same second, and I swear you could feel the electricity shoot between them from the other side of the fire. It was pretty obvious that none of the other guys had a chance with Lila once Johnny came into the picture, so they stopped their ridiculous posturing and started pairing off with the other girls.

I got up and walked to the far end of the fire, as far away from the rest as I could get without being obvious. I'd never felt so out of place in my life. Everyone, even Jeff, was with someone. Then, when I was trying to figure out if I could sneak back to the car without anyone seeing me, Ray came up behind me and sat down. He had a couple of raw wieners in his hand and offered me one. When I took it from him our hands touched, and I felt the stump where his little finger once grew. I jumped like I'd hit a live electric socket and, of course, dropped the wiener in the sand. Raymond calmly picked it up, dusted it off and gave it back to me with his other hand. My embarrassment was now complete. I stuck the wiener into the flames and prayed for a painless death.

The rest of the evening remains a blur. I sat on the sidelines watching Lila and envying her so much my teeth hurt. She was everything I ever wanted to be and more. How, I wondered, could two people come from the same family and be so different?

At least I wasn't left alone. Ray, probably at Jeff's insistence, stayed with me the whole evening and tried to make me feel comfortable. He told me about the chess tournament he had been in the week before and how he had made third place. I can't stand checkers, let alone chess, so I guess I wasn't too responsive. He talked about the boat he was building and the course he was taking in aircraft recognition and about a million other fascinating topics. I answered in grunts and felt stupid. Finally it was time to head for home.

Everyone started walking dreamily to their cars in pairs while Raymond and I gathered up the blankets and doused the fire. I knew I had been a complete pill and was feeling horrible.

"Ray, it was really super of you to stay with me tonight. I'm sorry if it was a drag for you." Averting my eyes, I threw the remains of a sand-covered hot dog into the fire. "I guess I feel a little out of my depth with all you older guys."

Raymond gave me a big grin and ruffled my hair.

"I understand, Hope. But remember, you're only a couple of years younger than most of us. And you're about ten times as smart."

"Yeah, sure. Straight A student; straight Z girl."

"Not true. Looks aren't everything, you know. Not that you're not real cute," he added hastily. "I just mean you don't have to look like Lila to be special."

I looked at him in disbelief. Did I really hear him say he thought I was cute?

Then he put the topping on the cake by adding, "How would you like to go to the movies with me next Saturday night?"

Now, you must understand something. In Kamloops, B.C., population not quite 8,000, there is one movie theatre, and everyone who is over thirteen and sighted goes to it on the weekend. It's the big entertainment centre for the city. Afterwards, everyone who was at the movie goes to the Top Hat cafe or McNeil's. It's a tradition. So, needless to say, everyone over thirteen and sighted would see me with Raymond Rounds. Hope Elise Mather with a real date!

Then I remembered the party for Anna's relatives. It was going to be on Saturday night too. I could hardly not show when it was going to be at my own house. I wondered if anyone else in the entire North American continent had such lousy luck.

"Gee, I'm sorry, Ray. I'd really love to, but we're having this party for some people who are new in town."

"Okay. Maybe some other time."

I thought of asking him if he'd like to come to the party, but I was afraid he'd think I was chasing him. Besides, I may be paranoid, but I thought he sounded relieved when I turned down the movie. But then, what else could I expect? He probably only asked me because he felt sorry for Jeff's ugly duckling sister.

He helped me carry my blanket up to the car, where we found Jeff and some girl already inside.

Lila and Johnny were standing beside Johnny's Hudson, and when we came in sight, Lila called over to me.

"Want to drive home with us, Hope? It's a lot more comfortable than that rumble seat of Jeff's."

I would rather have crawled the five miles to the city pushing a pea with my nose than have to be the third wheel, but I knew either Lila or Jeff would insist. I figured riding with my brother would be the least embarrassing, so I shook my head and started toward the coupe.

"I'll drive you home, Hope." Raymond took my hand and led me past the cars lined up in the driveway to an old red pickup truck. "Hop in," he ordered, opening the passenger door.

Gratefully I stepped on the running board and slipped inside. Ray closed the door and walked around to the driver's side.

"I'm sorry about the truck. It's not very comfortable," he apologized as he started the motor.

I smiled and shook my head. "It's super," I said, and I meant it. As I glanced at him out of the corner of my eye, I wondered if Jeff had really asked him to look out for me. Or was it just possible that it was Ray's own idea?

*   *   *

44

I woke up the next day to the welcome pounding of rain on the sleeping porch roof. It sounded like it was planning to stay for the day, so I rolled over and tried to recapture the dream I had been having. Clark Gable just wasn't about to make a return appearance, however, so I finally gave up and struggled into a sitting position.

We had pushed our beds out onto the porch off our bedroom when we got home last night, trying to get a little cool breeze. I looked over and saw that Lila was already up and obviously dressed since her pyjamas were neatly folded on her perfectly made bed. I pulled my nightie over my head and looked down at my oversized stomach. Why on earth would anyone be interested in you? I mocked my imaginings of last night. Discouraged, I threw my legs over the edge of the bed and got up.

In the bedroom, I looked into the dressing table mirror. The three volunteer pimples of yesterday were about twice their original size, and two more had joined them. No possible reason in the universe, I assured that glum face, then rubbed a good big blob of cold cream on the whole mess and went down to the bathroom to wash.

Lila and Mom were at the kitchen table when I got downstairs. The smell of fresh waffles and frying bacon was making my stomach rumble, so I just said a quick "Hi!" and started loading my plate. As I sat down, I saw Mom glance at Lila and shake her head. I ignored her and reached for the maple syrup pitcher.

"Hope, dear, don't you think you ought to go easy on that sweet stuff?" Mom said gently.

I looked down at my plate and saw that I'd poured about a cup of syrup on the waffles. But so what? Waffles aren't any good without lots of syrup. I picked up my knife and fork and cut into the three-tiered stack. Then, just as I began to stuff it into my mouth, I glanced over at Lila's plate: one waffle, no syrup, two strips of very crisp bacon. Suddenly I felt like a disgusting two-year-old shoving candy in its greedy mouth. I put down the fork full of food and got up from the table.

"I just remembered a phone call I have to make," I mumbled as I hurried out of the room.

What was the matter with me anyway? Why did I have to make such a pig of myself, especially in front of Lila? I could find excuses for the chocolate bars I ate for depression, but did I have to fill my plate like a starving rhino at every meal? No wonder I looked like I did. I sat on the stairs in the hall and cried.

Lila found me there a few minutes later. She didn't make any big deal about the tears — pretended to not see them. Instead, she sat down beside me and put her arm around me.

"It looks like it's going to rain all day," she remarked. "Maybe we can play a game or something later on."

I gave her a grateful look and answered, "Aren't you going to see Johnny La Longa?"

"Not till tonight," she answered. "He's taking me to Paul Lake for a boat ride. How's that for romantic?"

"Fantastic!" I answered. "You really like him, don't you, Lila?"

"Well, I've just met him. But, yes, I think he's very nice."

"Nice?"

"Okay, terrific. But I don't intend to get involved. Having one man I care about missing in action is plenty."

She stood up and flicked her hand across her eyes determinedly.

"Let's get the dishes done. I have to press out a few things, then we can have that game if you like."

"That's swell," I agreed. "And we can make fudge to go with it," I added without thinking.

She walked into the kitchen and started filling the sink without answering me. Then, as she started handing me wet plates to dry, she said, "We can make fudge if you like, but I don't eat candy any more."

I remembered what she had told me last night and felt like a complete nut. Of course she didn't eat candy. But then, she probably hadn't been an addict.

"Did you find it hard to give up all the things that really taste good?" I asked.

"At first, yes, but it wasn't too hard really. Rationing had just come in and everyone had stopped using sugar unnecessarily. Chocolate bars were impossible to find. By the time I realized that the ration coupons gave us all the sugar we could use and candy was back on the market, I had beaten the craving."

I didn't say anything and we finished the dishes in silence.

"Well, I'll see you later, Hope," she said, finally drying her hands on her apron. "Think about what game you want to play."

I thought, but not about any game. Maybe, just maybe, I could do what Lila did. It wouldn't be easy, but surely I could at least give it a try. I thought about how many candy bars I went through in a week — I managed to stock up on them even though they were still hard to come by — and I was shocked. Then there were the cakes and the sundaes and sodas. I absently reached for the cookie jar and took out half a dozen shortbreads. If I could just cut down a little, maybe my skin would clear up and I might even lose a few pounds. I munched on the cookie and closed my eyes.

* * *

"If you'll just turn your head a little this way, Hope, I can get a three-quarter shot."

I turned my head obligingly and Max Factor gave me an encouraging nod.

"She's got the most beautiful complexion I've ever seen," I heard him whisper to the assistant who was sitting beside him watching the shooting of the commercial. "Ever since we made her the Max Factor Girl our sales have shot up."

"Every woman in the country thinks that if she uses our products, she'll look like Hope, I guess."

"Our cosmetics are wonderful," Max said, "but nothing could create a skin like hers. A woman has to be born with it. And have you noticed that figure? Her waist makes Scarlett O'Hara's look downright thick."

"Okay, honey, that's all for today." The photographer gave me a thumbs up salute.

I smiled over at Max and ran my fingers across my cheek. It felt like . . .

*   *   *

. . . cookie crumbs!

I looked down at my other hand and saw that I had eaten all of the shortbreads. I hadn't even tasted them! It was definitely time to do something drastic.

I went down the basement, where I found Lila ironing a white eyelet blouse.

"Oh, Hope, you startled me." She swung around, lifting the iron off the board.

"I'm sorry, but I need to talk to you."

"Sure, what about?"

"It's my weight and my skin. Do you think you could help me do something about them?"

She picked the blouse up and hung it on a hanger.

"Absolutely. I've been hoping you might get an urge to bring out the 'real you.'"

"I just hope the 'real me' is better than the

50

one we're now witnessing," I told her. "On the other hand, it sure couldn't be worse."

"Don't put yourself down so much, Hope. You're not nearly as bad as you think. You've got a lot going for you. It just needs a little nudge."

"So where do we start?"

"Let's go upstairs and we'll make some plans. I'm nearly finished here anyway." She unplugged the iron and lifted the ironed garments down from the clothes tree. I couldn't help but notice the two big skirts with the wide waist bands. They were about twenty inches around.

Upstairs she hung up her clothes, sat down on the edge of the dressing table and looked at me.

"First, the diet. No soft drinks, candy bars, gooey desserts, cookies, cake or fried foods. That should do it for starters. Eat as much fruit and vegetables as you like, but take it easy on the starches. Then for the skin care regime. Wash your face twice a day with green liquid soap — you can get it at the drugstore. It doesn't have any stuff like perfume added to it. And don't use any of that heavy cream; put calamine lotion on the spots instead. Your skin should clear up in a few days, and the pounds will drop off like magic. Oh, and wash your hair every night too. I guess I can't persuade you to pull it back off your face right now, but at least keep it really clean. After we've got you thinned down a little and your complexion looking great, we'll work on your clothes."

"That sounds like it would be super, but I really doubt that I'll be able to keep away from sweets. I'm a junkie, you know. Maybe I should just ease off, so as not to give my system too much of a shock."

"Not on your life. Cold turkey — that's the only way. If you're really serious, the time to start is now."

I sighed and thought of the beautiful layer cake that was sitting in the frig. Then I thought of the hideous layer of fat that was sitting on my hips. The fat won.

"Okay, as of this minute, no more fattening food. I'm going to be a size ten again even if it kills me."

"When was the last time you were a size ten, Hope?"

I went over to the closet and looked inside. A minute later I backed out and turned to face Lila who was waiting for my answer.

"I think it was when I was nine and a half."

We both cracked up.

Chapter 4
Impressing Troy

I started work at McNeil's the next day, a split shift: eleven to one-thirty and eight-thirty to eleven. I also started my French lessons with M. Lasseur. I'm not sure which was the more painful.

I don't think I've mentioned yet why I was taking French that summer in the first place. You see, Mom's best friend from college married a French Canadian and lived in Quebec City. She had invited me to spend the next July with her family. Kind of a cultural exchange, I guess. She had a couple of kids about my age who didn't speak any English, and they were coming to stay with us in August. I had taken French in junior high but I couldn't speak a word, so Mom decided to hire a tutor to bring me to the point where I could at least ask to have the butter passed.

I don't know where she found M. Lasseur, but I suspect it was in a social club for tyrants.

He barely spoke to me that first day, other than to shout at me when I pronounced a word incorrectly. And the homework he laid on was monumental. I tried to tell him I only wanted to learn to speak the language, not write it, and he darn near blew me across the room with his snort.

"You want to learn the language, you study grammar. Comprenez?"

I told him I comprenned, and he just shook his head in horror.

Then he asked me to translate a passage from Maupassant so he could see just how much I knew, but just after I got started he seemed to lose interest and sat staring at a big map of Europe that hung on the wall beside the blackboard. I think I could have broken into Chinese and he would merely have nodded, "Tres bien."

It wasn't till much later that month that I found out what was wrong with him.

When I went in to work later that morning I wore high-heeled wedges and rayon stockings, thinking they would make me look older and more sophisticated. After two hours I was walking on my ankles and envying people in wheel chairs. I didn't get to sit down once in that first shift, and by the time one o'clock came I was ready to throw in the towel.

I think I would have too, if Troy Farnham hadn't come in for a late lunch. He was wearing black denims and a white shirt that showed off both his tan and his incredible pectorals. His sandy hair was kind of ruffled and a lock hung down over his forehead. He looked good enough to bronze.

Gerry McNeil and I shared the workload alone even in rush hour. The only other waitress he had was his wife and she only worked on Saturdays. It was impossible for him to get more help — everyone who was over eighteen and breathing had left town to work in a munitions plant or joined up. That's how come I got the job in the first place, even though I was legally underage.

Usually I took the booths and Gerry manned the counter and the till. But that first day he had me on the counter so I could learn how to ring up cash in case he wasn't available. That's why I was able to wait on Troy, and for two or three minutes practically breathe the same air. I walked over to him almost in a daze.

"I'd like a ham and tomato sandwich on white, no dressing," he ordered with a smile that steamed up my glasses. "And a root beer shake."

I wrote the order down carefully and proceeded to try to fill it. The sandwich went together without too much trouble, but the shake was a disaster. When I put it on the beater to mix it, I inadvertently put my other hand on the metal ice cream bin underneath and got a shock that would light up London.

The shake shot out of my hand and landed in a brown puddle in Troy's lap. Horror took over my autonomic nervous system and I stopped breathing. I guess I also stopped pumping blood, because Gerry rushed over and led me to the back where he pushed me into a chair.

"Don't take it so hard, Hope. You're as white as a sheet. It was just an accident," he reassured me as he pushed a glass of water in my face. "Actually the whole thing's my fault. I should have had that faulty shake machine fixed ages ago."

He kind of patted my arm and muttered something about me staying back here until I felt better. Then he left to placate Troy.

Since there wasn't a back way out, I had no choice but to follow him a few minutes later. Troy was mopping his pants with a wet cloth and muttering to himself. I slipped in behind the counter and debated throwing myself at his feet. He must have seen my expression, because after one rueful glance at his pants he gave me another glass-steaming grin and said, "Don't worry about it. I've got the worst of it out and the cleaners will get the rest."

I was about to offer to pay for it when the door opened and Lila walked in. Troy didn't see her until she sat down a couple of stools away. Then his hand with the wet cloth paused in midair and he kind of collapsed back onto the stool. He didn't say anything. He didn't have to.

"Are you about ready to go home, Hope?" Lila asked, ignoring the panting beside her. "I've got something great to tell you."

I looked inquiringly at Gerry. He nodded and I escaped into the back again, where I took off my apron and slumped back onto the chair. I was filled with such a mixture of conflicting emotions I couldn't get them sorted out. However, embarrassment and envy seemed to be vying for top billing. After a moment or two I stood up, looked at myself in the cracked mirror over the sink, then turned and took three Cadbury chocolate bars from the box on the shelf and stuffed them in my purse. I went back into the cafe and slipped fifteen cents into the till, then came around to the other side of the counter. Lila and Troy were sitting side by side laughing. Probably at me, I decided.

"I'm ready," I muttered, trying not to sound as sulky as I felt. "Let's get out of here." I flung open the door and rushed outside. Lila caught up with me as I was crossing the street.

"What happened? Why are you so upset?" she gasped as I stopped and leaned against the brick wall of the bank building on the corner.

"Never mind," I answered grimly and started up the hill.

She didn't say anything, just plodded alongside of me looking worried. Then, after a block of silence, she spoke.

"Hope, guess what? I've been hired by the city for Johnny's job as lifeguard. Isn't that great?"

"Lifeguard? You?" I cried. "How did you manage that?"

"Well, I went down to the park early this morning to meet Johnny before he went on duty at ten. When he found out about my certificates, he suggested I apply for the job. So I did and I got it. Isn't that amazing?"

Not really, I thought to myself. Why wouldn't she land the most sought-after job in town? I could imagine what happened when she went to see the guy in personnel. He probably would have hired her if she'd had lead feet.

I *was* happy for her, or at least I was trying to be. Jealousy is a rotten emotion, one that I didn't think I'd ever really have. But it seemed like my cousin was bringing out the worst in me. It wasn't her fault, of course — she was a terrific person. It was me who wasn't so terrific. I should have been grateful that I had a job myself, instead of envying Lila hers.

"I'm going to start tomorrow," she was babbling on. "Johnny leaves on Thursday, so that will give us a couple of days for me to learn the ropes. I'm on duty weekdays from ten to six, so we'll still have the weekends together and evenings until you have to leave for the night shift. We can — " She stopped and looked at me. "Come on, Hope, tell me what's the matter. You look like someone just ran over your cat."

I tried to smile, but the day had finally gotten to me. My feet were so sore I could hardly walk, and the whole business with Troy and the shake and Lila was just too much. I leaned against the hot cement wall beside me and started to bawl.

"Hope, honey! What's happened? Please tell me."

I bent over and took off my shoes. The blister on my right foot was threatening to take over my whole leg, and the one on my left had already broken and was oozing blood all over my stocking, which was in folds around my ankle. My hair was plastered to my face and my glasses had slipped down to their usual spot on the end of my nose. My cotton dress was wet under the arms and splitting down the back seam. I slid down into a sitting position and stared at my feet. Then I told her about the fiasco with the milk shake.

"I'm such a mess and I'll never be anything but a mess," I finished. "I was born with mess genes, and there's nothing I can do about it."

She started to laugh, then seeing my face, sobered up.

"You're not a mess, Hope. Your feet, yes; Troy's pants, maybe; but not you."

I grinned in spite of myself. "I wish you could convince the rest of the human race about that." I blew my nose on a tired hanky and pushed my glasses back in place. "Come on, let's go. I've got a million verbs to memorize before I have to go back to work."

"Are you sure you can walk home? I could run ahead and get Aunt Prue's car, then come back for you."

"I'm all right now that the shoes are off."

"Well, okay, if you really think you can make it."

We walked the rest of the way in silence. When we got to the front of our house, I turned to her and said, "If only I looked like you, Lila, everything would be perfect."

"That's crazy. Looks never made anything perfect. But you are going to look great. Four weeks from now you'll be a different person."

Four weeks. Surely I could hold out that long. I thought of the chocolate bars in my purse and how they were going to make me feel so much better. Or were they? Chocolate gave me a great lift for a while, but then before an hour passed I'd start feeling even lower than before. It couldn't be doing me much good. I wasn't really buying this "different person" bit that Lila was giving me, but I could at least give it a try.

"Fours week, eh? Okay, why not?"

Lila put her arm around my shoulder, and as we walked up the steps to the front porch said, "Look, as an incentive, if you can get down to your ideal weight in four weeks, I'll buy you the sexiest bathing suit they've got at the Bay."

"You're on. And if I don't make it, I'll give you my last year's sharkskin number with the skirt."

"My God," she groaned, "in that case you've *got* to make it!"

She moved ahead of me to open the door, and I slipped my hand into my purse, took out the chocolate bars and quickly tossed them behind the lilac bush.

* * *

Somehow I managed to get through the evening shift that night with a minimum of pain. I traded my high heels for a pair of old sandals, and bandaged the blisters. My feet looked like they came right out of a sarcophagus, but at least I could walk without limping.

My shift began at eight-thirty, but the crowd didn't descend until after nine when the movie got out. So the place was almost deserted when Anna came in with Marie and three strangers.

They sat down at a booth, and when I went over to take their orders, Anna introduced me.

"Hope, I'd like you to meet our cousins: Sue, Thomas and Lyle Takada. This is my best friend, Hope Mather."

I looked down at the three kids lined up on one side of the booth and wondered again about the genetic dice throw. The two boys were dolls; Sue was, to put it kindly, plain. She had straight black hair that didn't look like it was happy living on her head, and I would bet anything that she could crack walnuts with her overbite. It was just like in my family — the boy got the looks, the girl got zip.

"Lyle will be in our grade, Hope, and Thomas goes into nine."

"What about you, Sue? Are you in junior high too?"

"No, I graduated last June. I'm leaving for Ontario soon. I'm hoping they'll let me join the WACs there. Or if not I might go on down to the States and see if I can get into their armed forces. I can't do anything here in B.C., of course."

I stared at her in disbelief. She didn't look old enough to be crossing the street by herself, let alone trying so hard to join the army.

I guess she saw my expression because she started to laugh.

"I turned eighteen last month," she told me. "I know I don't look it though. It's been a problem all my life. When I used to baby-sit our eight-year-old cousin, people were always asking which one of us was the sitter."

She might be strange looking, but at least she had a sense of humour.

I took their order, and when I brought it to

them, Anna moved over and asked me to sit down. There weren't any other customers, so I grabbed a glass of tomato juice and slid into the booth beside her.

Anna looked at my juice then at me. "What, no chocolate malt?"

I didn't want to tell anyone about my diet just yet, so I made a face and said, "Oh, I'm up to here with ice cream and stuff. I couldn't eat another bite."

She gave me a concerned look and said, "Are you sure this is the best place for you to be, Hope?"

"I'll wear all the calories off running around during rush hour," I assured her. Then I turned to Marie and asked, "Did you tell them about the party?"

"I mentioned it, but I didn't know when you planned to have it."

"Saturday, if that's okay with you. It won't be big, just us and Lila and Jeff. I'll ask Shirley, but I doubt if she'll come."

"We'll be there," Anna answered.

I smiled and drank the rest of my juice. "The crowd will be piling in any time, so I'd better get back to my post," I announced, struggling up on my wounded feet. "See you Saturday, if not before." I wondered what Jeff would say when he saw Sue. I knew he liked his girls to be, if not Lila calibre, at least mildly gorgeous. I hoped he wouldn't let his feelings show.

When I got home at eleven, Lila was sitting cross-legged in her pyjamas and looking very pleased with herself. As I came into our room, she pulled a huge paper bag with the Hudson's Bay logo on it from behind her back.

"I've got a surprise for you," she grinned, opening the bag. Out came yards of material and a collection of pattern books. "I decided that you were going to need a whole new wardrobe to fit your new figure, so Aunt Prue and I went shopping this afternoon."

I ran over to the bed and stared at the bright cotton fabrics that lay there.

"But I'm a rotten sewer!" I cried.

"I'm not. And you can learn. We'll start with broomstick skirts; they don't even take a pattern. Then we'll make up three or four dresses. Do you like the material we chose?" She didn't wait for me to answer, but continued excitedly. "We'll pick out patterns together and Aunt Prue will get them for us. We can start on the broomsticks when you get home from work tomorrow. In fact, we can probably get one done right now."

She pulled a tape measure out of the bag and instructed me to strip down to my panties and bra. As she put the tape measure around me, I sucked in my stomach. "Wow! Thirty inches!" she exclaimed. "Never mind, we'll make the bands smaller and plan on you losing a few inches. A lot of that is just water and should go quickly." I hate to think how she would have reacted if I *hadn't* sucked in my stomach.

Before I knew what was happening, Lila was ripping material and doing clever things with a needle. After about fifteen minutes, she left the room and went down to the basement where Mom keeps an old sewing machine. She was back before I had completed my nightly ritual of hair washing, green soap scrubbing and calamine lotion smearing.

"There. Now all we have to do is hem it and sew on the hooks and eyes."

It was lovely: red, green, blue and white stripes going around the band and vertically down the skirt. The waist looked about big enough to fit my arm.

"I love it, Lila," I sighed, "but I'll never in a million years be able to wear it."

"Of course you will. Now climb into bed before your folks come in here and ground us for life." She jumped into her bed and turned out her bedside light. "We can work weekends and afternoons for now. I don't start at the park full-time till Thursday. We'll have a terrific wardrobe ready in time for your debut."

I believed her for about five minutes. Then, as I started to drift off to sleep, a great big chocolate-coated marshmallow began chasing me around the room crying, "Eat me! Eat me!" I wondered how long I could hold out.

Chapter 5
Party time

I spent that first week of Operation Diet tearing around like a demented rabbit. I barely had time to eat breakfast before Lila had me out on the porch doing sit-ups and knee bends and about a million other little muscle stretchers that rivalled the rack for torture. The first day I nearly ended up at Digger O'Dell's mortuary, but by the end of the week I was almost able to move without screaming and had more energy than I'd had since I was two.

I soon began to get the hang of my job too. I stopped electrocuting myself on the milk shake machine and got so I could take cash almost as fast as Gerry. I even managed to gain some control over my salivary glands when I smelled chocolate syrup. I hadn't had a grain of sugar since Sunday, and I was definitely suffering from withdrawal. I doubt if I could have kept up the good work if it hadn't been for thinking about Troy. I was hoping Jeff would ask him to the party on Saturday, and I was determined to at least get control of the acne before then.

I hadn't told anyone about my big crush — there wasn't anyone to tell. Shirley hadn't let anyone talk about boys since she got fat and decided to be a career woman, Anna was preoccupied with her cousins, and Lila was preoccupied with Johnny. He left on Thursday and she spent Friday in mourning.

Saturday finally arrived and was I glad to see it. I didn't have French on the weekends, but I did have to put in the noon shift at McNeil's. Still, I was able to sleep until the decadent hour of nine o'clock before Lila had me up and helping her crank the ice cream maker. Even though the temperature was back in the mid-nineties, we lit the stove and made two cakes and three batches of cookies. For the first time that week, I was glad to be going to work at the soda fountain.

It looked like it was going to be my lucky day. Troy came in about one o'clock. As I walked carefully over to take his order, I hoped this might be my chance to make a better impression. Then Laurie McVale, the town flirt, came in and sat beside him. Any hopes I had that maybe Jeff had asked him to the party were thoroughly dashed when I overheard them talking about going out to Paul Lake together. I wasn't too upset about him being with Laurie though — every guy in town had taken her out at least once. You could say that dating Laurie was the Kamloops version of a coming-of-age ceremony.

However, one thing did upset me. When I took their orders to them, Laurie looked me up and down and, in a voice you could hear in Alaska, commented, "My, that apron is attractive, Hope. It does wonders to hide your hips and stomach."

Troy didn't say anything, but the look he gave Laurie would freeze steam.

I slapped their bill down without saying anything and went into the back of the shop.

I looked in the cracked mirror and pulled my bangs away from my face. The pimples were definitely drying up, and there had been no new eruptions since Sunday. I still looked like I'd been bitten by killer ants, but Lila assured me that the scars would fade quickly. I ran my hands down over my stomach and hips. Not so encouraging. I couldn't feel my hipbones and the stomach bulges were still hanging in there. I eyed the boxes of chocolate bars longingly. Just one to take the bad taste of Laurie's remark away. I snatched a Dairy

Milk out of the box, tore the paper off and took a huge bite. The chocolate felt like sweet velvet as I swirled it around my mouth before swallowing it. I took another bite. And another. In about fifteen seconds, the bar had disappeared. I stood looking at the empty wrapper and hating myself. Then, like a replay of Vesuvius, my stomach gave an awesome rumble and the chocolate came right back up. I made it to the sink just in time. It wasn't nearly as tasty the second time around. I washed out my mouth, wiped the perspiration off my forehead and went back out into the shop completely discouraged. Even my stomach had turned against me.

I got home to find Lila sitting on the floor in the living room, surrounded by stacks of records and unpacking her pick-up. She had brought it with her from Vancouver along with a bunch of Decca records we couldn't buy in Kamloops. It was a new kind of phonograph that operated through the radio, so instead of having to wind up the machine after every record, you just started it and it kept going. Now if only someone would invent something that would change the records automatically — but I guess that would be asking too much.

She finally got the thing attached to the back

of the radio and put on my favourite Glenn Miller song, "String of Pearls." I stayed till the record ended, then left her on the floor sorting records and went upstairs to shower and lie down before getting ready for the party. I wondered what I could possibly wear that wouldn't make me look like Lou Costello in drag, and decided on a pair of shorts and a white shirt of Dad's. It was supposed to be casual, and the shirt would cover my bulges almost as well as the apron at work. Not that it mattered much what I looked like. No one would see me but Jeff and the Takada brothers, and they were too young.

Somehow all my excitement about the party had disappeared. The thought of a trip to Paul Lake with Troy made it seem like a day at the dentist in comparison. I rolled over on my stomach and tried to erase the memory of Laurie's remark about my apron. In a couple of minutes I was fast asleep.

I hoped I would at least dream about Troy, but no such luck. Instead, I spent the next hundred years running around a record that wouldn't stop spinning, and chasing a Cadbury chocolate bar with buck teeth.

*　　*　　*

I must have been more exhausted than I realized. When I finally woke up, I could hear music from downstairs and a lot of people talking at once.

I jumped up from the bed and threw on my shorts and shirt, wondering why nobody had bothered to wake me. A quick comb through my hair and a damp cloth over my glasses and I was ready. I considered putting on a little lipstick, but decided it would only direct attention to my still spotty face. I did pat a little pancake make-up on though, and was surprised at how much it actually camouflaged.

Downstairs the party was in full swing. Someone had moved all the furniture against the living room wall, and couples were dancing to Lila's records. I looked around and was surprised to see that Shirley had decided to come after all. The Suzukis and Takadas were all there, all except Sue. Marie had brought her boyfriend, and his brother Billy had come along too — much to Anna's obvious delight — so there was quite a crowd.

When Lila saw me, she stopped dancing with Thomas Takada and came over to where I was standing in the entrance to the hall.

"Oh, Hope, you're up," she smiled. "We debated about waking you sooner, but your mom thought you needed the sleep. You looked beat when you came home from work."

"Yeah, I guess I must have been. How's the party going?"

"Great. You haven't missed too much of it though. Aren't the Takada boys adorable?"

"Yeah, they're adorable all right." I looked over to where Thomas was gazing at Lila like a stranded puppy and laughed.

"You seem to have made a deep impression on the baby of the family."

"He was so shy," Lila explained with a grin. "And I really don't think Johnny would be too jealous, do you?"

"I don't know," I teased, "he looks awfully taken. By the way" — I looked around the room — "where's Jeff? He didn't sneak out on us, did he?"

"He's out on the porch dancing with Sue."

"Oh, good. I'm glad he's making the effort to be nice. Isn't it a darn shame?"

Lila looked baffled. "Isn't what a darn shame?"

"Her looks, of course. That hair and the overbite. Even her eyes are kind of odd."

Lila gave me a strange look and said, "Jeff doesn't seem to be put off by her odd eyes and

overbite. He's been with her ever since she arrived."

"Really?" I exclaimed. "How weird."

The record finished and Lila left to change it.
The Suzukis and their dates came over to say hi,
then Thomas Takada asked me for the next
dance.

I'm five foot three, but Thomas came just up
to my chin. At first I wanted to refuse. Then I
remembered that Lila was a good four inches
taller than me and the difference in heights
hadn't bothered her. I still felt uncomfortable, but
I struggled through.

When the record ended, I excused myself and
went to the kitchen — a reflex action, I suppose. I
looked at all the food Mom had laid out and had
to restrain my right hand from reaching for the
chocolate cookies. I wanted to stay in the safety of
the room, but I knew that, as hostess, I'd have to
go back out and be friendly. I hoped the Takadas
were having a good time — after all, the party
was for them. As far as I was concerned, it was a
dead loss.

While I was sitting there talking myself into
returning to the party, I heard a knock on the
back door. Probably old Mrs. Quick from next
door complaining about the noise, I thought. I

went to open it all ready to apologize, but it wasn't Mrs. Quick. It was Raymond Rounds.

"Hi, Hope. Sorry I'm late, but the front tire sprung a leak just after I crossed the bridge and the spare was flat."

I stood there blocking the door and looking at him like he was General Patton come to borrow a cup of sugar.

"What are you doing here?" I demanded.

"Well, isn't there a party going on? Jeff said to come about seven."

"Jeff invited you? Why?"

He started to laugh and shoved his hands in his pockets.

"Gee, it's nice to feel wanted. Are you going to block the door all night, or could I maybe come in for a couple of minutes?"

I realized how I must have sounded and blushed right down to my semi-healed blisters.

"Ray, I'm sorry." I stared down at my feet and moved away from the door. He grinned and walked past me into the kitchen.

"Wow, look at all that fabulous food! I knew there was something drawing me here tonight."

His back was turned to me so I couldn't see the expression on his face. Gluttony, no doubt. I was thinking seriously of picking up the dish of pickled beets and pouring them over his head when he turned around. Seeing the expression on my face, he burst out laughing.

"Hope, I was kidding. I came because Jeff asked me — and because I knew you would be here."

"Oh, come on," I answered brilliantly, and wondered what had happened to the rest of my vocabulary.

"Shall we go in where the dancing is or would you rather just stay here and watch the chocolate icing melt?" Without waiting for an answer, he put his hand on my shoulder and half pushed me through the door.

Someone had dimmed the lights, and four couples were moving slowly to the haunting sounds of Duke Ellington. Lila was nowhere in sight, and Thomas sat alone on the couch methodically working his way to the bottom of the peanut dish. The Suzukis had switched partners and Jeff and Sue were pasted together like they were magnetized. Shirley and Lyle Takada looked as though they were trying to decide which one of them should lead and not coming up with an answer. It was an arresting sight, to say the least.

Ray put out his arms and I stumbled into

them. As he pulled me close, I sucked in my stomach so it wouldn't push against him and quickly wiped my wet palms on the tail of my shirt. My glasses had slipped down to their usual place on the end of my nose, and as Ray tucked my head on his shoulder, they slid off and hung from my left ear. I didn't dare try to straighten them, so I spent the first romantic dance of my life in a total blur.

The party really was a great success. About eleven we all piled into the kitchen and dove into the food — all, that is, but Jeff and Sue. They had left sometime between Duke Ellington and Artie Shaw, and no one had seen them since. Shirley and Lyle seemed to hit it off pretty well too. He didn't seem to mind her rather hefty bulk, and she obviously didn't care that he was the same age as her.

Ray asked Lila to dance a couple of times, and each time I retreated to the kitchen. I just didn't want anyone to see me dancing with little Thomas or sitting alone. It never occurred to me that one of the Suzukis' dates would probably have asked me to dance; I'd been too conditioned by my experience at school mixers.

I had fun with Ray though, after I got over my clumsiness. He was a great dancer — he made me feel positively feathery. And he was great to talk to. Before we had danced two dances we were gabbing away like we were long lost cousins who hadn't seen each other for fifty years. The only fly in the ointment, as they say, was his little finger — or actually the lack of it. I had to hold his left hand when we danced, of course, and I couldn't bear to touch the stump. So I somehow managed to wind my fingers around his wrist and pretend that was the perfectly normal position. Ray went along with it and didn't say anything, but I couldn't help feel embarrassed and kind of ashamed.

Jeff and Sue came home about one, and the party broke up shortly after. Ray offered to stay and help clean up, but I insisted he go home; he had farther to drive than anyone else, and I knew how unreliable old retreads were.

He asked me to walk him to his truck, much to the amusement of both Lila and Jeff. He had parked in the lane behind the house, and when we got to it, he turned to me and said, "It was fun, Hope. Better than a movie would have been."

I remembered he had asked me at the wiener roast to go out with him tonight.

"I'm glad you had a good time," I answered, and held my breath. Would he ask me again?

"So how about next Saturday then?" he said right on cue. "*The White Cliffs of Dover* is coming and I'm an Irene Dunne nut."

"Me too," I answered, and let my breath out with a whoosh that nearly knocked him over. Oh, I was smooth, all right!

"Well? Will you go then?"

Would I go? Would I like to take a trip to Paris? Would I accept a movie contract with MGM? Would I model gowns for Dior?

"Sure, okay," I answered, trying for a nonchalance that didn't quite come off.

"Great. I'll pick you up about six-forty-five." He gave me a peck on the cheek, jumped into his truck and drove off.

I leaned against the fence and watched the tail-lights disappear down the alley. It was almost more than I could handle in one evening — a real date *and* a kiss. Well, sort of a kiss. I whirled around and danced back to the house.

Lila was alone in the kitchen putting the last of the food away when I came in. I started to help her, but she shooed me off to bed. I think she wanted to be alone for awhile. I told her I'd see her later and ran upstairs to get ready for bed.

It wasn't until I had washed my face, brushed my teeth and changed into my nightie that I thought about Troy Farnham. I wondered if he and Laurie were back from the lake, and what they were doing right now. Strangely, I didn't feel the resentment I had felt earlier in the cafe. My evening had been great too. Ray was a really neat guy — maybe not in Troy's class when it came to looks, but still okay. I might just as well make up my mind that the Troy Farnhams of the world were never going to be turned on by fat, ugly little Hope Mather, and be grateful that the Raymond Rounds weren't so fussy.

Chapter 6
A real date at last

I didn't have to wait till the following Saturday to see Ray. He and Sue Takada came for Sunday dinner. I don't know how it happened, because I slept in again Sunday morning. When I got downstairs at twelve-thirty, the whole family was coming home from church and Sue and Ray were with them. Jeff's offhand explanation was that they happened to meet them there and it just seemed natural for everyone to come home together.It was a nice try, but I happened to know the Suzukis were United Church, therefore the Takadas probably were too, and I had never seen Ray in the Anglican church in my entire life.

Anyway, it was fun to have them, not that Jeff or Sue contributed a whole lot to the merriment of the meal. They sat across the table from each other and exchanged sickly glances when they thought no one was watching. I couldn't understand Jeff at all — he was one of the most sought-after boys in Kamloops and there he was going overboard for a girl who looked like a chipmunk.

I didn't believe Ray was really interested in me, so I finally concluded the only possible reason for his attention was that he was hung up on Lila. Lila, on the other hand, was carrying a very bright torch for Johnny. Every male with facial hair spent the rest of that week trying to date her now that Johnny was gone, but she turned them all down.

Then Troy Farnham asked her out and she accepted. I'm sorry to say that when I heard that news it took a big bite out of my excitement over my date with Ray. Her date was on Saturday too. She was going to some sort of house party out in the country, which made Saturday night at the movies seem pretty boring. However, I kept reminding myself about beggars and choosers, and by the time Saturday rolled around most of the excitement had returned.

Ray had had a birthday the previous Wednesday, and his folks bought him a second-hand Master Deluxe Chevie. It was dark red and looked practically new. I have to admit I was awfully glad he didn't arrive in the family pickup. I was still hoping to make a big impression on all the kids who would see me with him at the show.

As it turned out, no one saw us at the show after all. We arrived late and had to sit in the back row, and when the movie was over, Ray had us out of the theatre before most people had retrieved their gum from under the seats.

When we got outside, he asked me if I'd like a drink. I was desperately thirsty from not having drunk anything since noon — I couldn't *imagine* having to go to the ladies' room in the middle of the picture — and besides, I wanted to be seen in the restaurant with a date, so I jumped at the offer.

"That would be super, Raymond. Let's leave the car here and walk — the Top Hat is only a couple of blocks." That would give anyone who was not in the cafe a chance to see me as well.

"Naw, that place is too crowded, Hope. Let's drive down to the Commodore where it's quiet and we can talk."

The car was parked right in front of the theatre, and before I could come up with a counter proposal, I was tucked beside him in the passenger seat.

Ray was right. The Commodore *was* quiet. We were the only customers. I followed him down the aisle to a booth in the back, and he stood aside for me to sit. Then he slid in across from me and smiled.

"Isn't this better than that cattle auction up the street?" he asked.

I thought of all the kids who had watched me spend every dance and party since grade school either in the washroom or cutting sandwiches in the kitchen. They were now at the Top Hat or McNeil's, and I was in the Commodore.

"Yeah, it's great," I muttered.

I guess Ray must have seen my depression because he started telling jokes. They were the worst jokes I'd ever heard. At first I was so embarrassed for him I wanted to crawl under my seat. But soon I realized that he knew as well as I did how bad the jokes were, and I began to laugh. The jokes got worse, and by the time our drinks had come I was practically hysterical.

After he'd finished his comedy routine, he ordered another round of sodas and started asking me about movies I liked.

"I think *Mrs. Miniver* is the most wonderful picture I've ever seen," I gushed. "And I adore Greer Garson."

"I don't know. I thought it was a little too sappy."

"It was not!" I countered indignantly, and the battle was on.

We went from movies to radio shows to school subjects without a single pause in the conversation. He was as easy and comfortable to talk to as Anna or Shirley.

By the time we'd put away four sodas each, it was nearly midnight. Ray was the first to notice the time.

"Gee, Hope, I'd better get you back home or your folks will have me up for kidnapping."

As I made a move to stand, I realized that the four bottles of pop weren't going to stay around too long. I guess I must have looked desperate, because Ray stood up and casually remarked, "I think I'll make a stop at the men's room before we go," and left me to rush to the ladies' without dying of shame.

He drove me directly home and walked me to the door. I had no idea how to behave under the circumstances. Should I stand there, waiting for him to kiss me good night? Or would I look stupid? Ray solved the problem by opening the door for me and kissing the top of my head.

"That was fun, Hope. We should do it again." He smiled and ran back down the steps to his car.

That's when the old self doubts began raising

their nasty heads. Was he being nice to me because Jeff had asked him to? Was he really trying to get to Lila? Or maybe he was a closet masochist and got his jollies from fat frumps. If he wasn't ashamed of me, why had he rushed out of the theatre before anyone saw us and then insisted we go to the most deserted cafe in town? I slumped into the house and upstairs, wondering if maybe I should plan to be a career woman like Shirley.

Lila was asleep when I came into the bedroom, but she woke up while I was undressing.

"Did you have a good time?" she asked sleepily.

"Yes. No. I don't know. Did you?"

"It was nice enough. The party's still going on, I guess, but I — "

I didn't wait to hear the rest, just threw my clothes in a heap on the floor and went down to the bathroom. I was brushing my teeth when I felt Lila behind me.

"Okay, what happened?" she demanded, leaning against the doorjamb and looking me over.

"Nothing happened. That's the trouble. He thinks I'm a jerk kid."

"Oh, Hope. Why do you put yourself down so

much? He likes you or he'd never have asked you out."

I swirled my mouth out and spit disgustedly.

"He just felt sorry for me because I'm so ugly. It was his volunteer work for the month of July. I think maybe he's got a thing for you and is try to get to you through me."

Lila burst out laughing. "That's the dumbest thing I've ever heard."

"Yeah? Then how come he didn't want to be seen with me? And what about the big good night kiss?" I started to wash my face, and between rinses gave her a rundown on the evening.

"Then he kissed me on the top of the head," I complained, wiping my face and patting on lotion. "How's that for romantic?"

"Don't knock it, Hope. Just be thankful he's not the other way."

"Yeah, well, maybe if I play my cards right he'll kiss me on the nose next time. In a couple of years, he might even make it to my mouth."

"Give it time," Lila answered, trying to keep the laughter under control. "How much will you bet that he calls for another date within the next three days?"

"You must want to lose your money," I grumbled. I put the lotion on the shelf and turned to leave the room. "Fifty cents — that's a whole week's allowance."

"You're on," she replied.

I gave her the half dollar the next afternoon.

*   *   *

The next week passed in a kind of hungry fog. I worked at the cafe at noon and in the evening, went to M. Lasseur for tutoring every morning, and studied in the afternoon. The rest of the time I sat around and thought thin.

If it hadn't been for Ray and Lila, I probably would have gone around the bend. Lila helped me sew my new wardrobe every evening before I had to go back to work, and we really got to know one another. It was her encouragement and her faith in me that kept me going even when I was ready to trade my left leg for a chocolate malt. I told her practically everything about me, stuff that I had never told anyone, not even Anna or Shirley. One night I even confided my secret crush on Troy Farnham. She hadn't been out with him since the Saturday of the house party. I don't know if he didn't ask her or whether she just decided he wasn't her type. When I asked her if she planned to date him again, she only shook her head and changed the subject.

As for Ray, he was terrific. He picked me up every night from work and drove me home, then we'd sit on the porch and talk until Mom started blinking the lights — her subtle way of telling him it was time for me to be in bed. He was fascinating to listen to. He read an awful lot; I suppose being on the farm and away from the "big city" life got him in the habit. Anyway, he knew something about almost everything, some of it a bit far-fetched. For instance, he told me that when the war was over, everyone would have something called television right in their living room. Like the radio only with pictures. He said it had been around since the thirties, but the war had stopped production of it. Honestly! And he expected me to believe him!

He taught me to play chess and offered to let me help sand and paint his boat when it was built. He even offered to teach me aircraft recognition, but I had to pass on that one. Even with my glasses I could hardly find the moon.

That Saturday he took me to the movies again. I was beginning to feel a lot more sure of myself with him and had almost abandoned the idea that he was secretly after Lila. I even suspected he might try to hold my hand during the show, so I had put lots of Etiquet antiperspirant on my palms before I left the house. I tried to arrange it so I would be sitting on his right side, but since we were ushered down the right aisle I had to go in first, which put me on his left. I didn't know how I would react to holding the hand with the missing finger, but I was determined not to let it show. I guess I didn't do very well.

We were sitting drinking lemonade on our front porch after the show when Ray said, "My finger — or the lack of it — really bothers you, doesn't it, Hope?"

"Oh, no. In fact I never even noticed."

He laughed and put his arm around my shoulder.

"Sure you didn't."

I didn't know what to say, and the silence was getting positively spooky when he continued in a more serious tone.

"I suppose this sounds corny, but the way people make such a big thing out of physical appearance really turns me off. I just can't see where a pretty face or a great body makes anyone so special." He started to laugh again. "Maybe that's because I've been around animals all my life, and I think there's nothing more beautiful than a pregnant sow."

I didn't know if he was joking or not, so I gave a half laugh and said nothing.

"Take you, for instance. I think you're really pretty, but I know you don't think so. All you see is your mirror. I see a lot more."

Now I was sure he was joking.

"Yeah, me and Ingrid Bergman. Two of a kind."

"Hope, I really meant — " He was leaning closer, and I had the distinct feeling he was going to make it to my mouth when the floodlight went on in the front yard. I guess Mom had got tired of blinking the hall light and was resorting to drastic measures to get me inside without actually hauling me in bodily. Her timing has always been impeccable.

Ray moved away and I breathed a small sigh. He gave a little shrug and said, "Guess that's my signal to let you go in. I'll see you next Saturday, okay?"

"Sure," I answered, and reached up and kissed him on the cheek. He raised his eyebrows, but he didn't say anything. I went into the house feeling completely confused and wondering why everyone said being a teenager was so much fun.

Chapter 7
Everything begins to unravel

The following week my relatively simple and happy life began to come disastrously apart. The first thing that happened didn't start out as a disaster, but it certainly was a change. It involved M. Lasseur.

I mentioned earlier that he normally spent our happy little tutoring sessions either yelling at me or ignoring me. I couldn't figure out what was the matter with him, so I put it down to the Gallic temperament I'd heard about. But it wasn't that at all.

On that Tuesday, July 25th — the date is engraved in indelible pencil on my brain — I went into his study without knocking and found him sitting in his rocking chair with his eyes closed. At first I thought he was asleep, which was strange in itself. He was usually standing at the blackboard writing a whole new list of impossible verbs for me to memorize and glancing at his watch to let me know I was seven seconds late. I went over to him and put my hand on his shoulder to wake him. It was then that I saw the tears streaming down his face. Without thinking, I knelt down on the floor beside his chair and took his hand. Neither of us spoke for at least five minutes. Finally he took his hand from mine and reached in his pocket for a handkerchief. He wiped his eyes and looked over at me with the saddest expression I'd ever seen.

"Thank you, cherie. You are a kind child," he said at last. "Perhaps you would not mind if we did not study today."

Mind? Would I mind if someone gave me a Studebaker convertible?

"Sure, that's okay," I answered, trying not to sound too pleased. Then, realizing that my pleasure seemed to be coming from his pain, I ventured a tentative, "Have you had bad news, M. Lasseur?"

"No, Hope. Not bad news. No news. I keep hoping every day . . . " He stopped and looked down at the handkerchief that he was twisting between his fingers. "But nothing, nothing at all is what I hear."

I waited, not knowing whether to leave or to

ask him what he meant. Before I could decide, he went on.

"When I came to your country in 1939, I left my wife and little son in Paris. I intended to send for them as soon as I had settled myself here. But the war broke out. I tried to get them out of France before she fell, but I could not manage it. I have not heard from my wife for almost a year now. I despair that great harm has befallen her. You see, she is Jewish."

I'd heard about the Germans and their death camps, but it was all like a movie to me — not real. I didn't know what to say. There wasn't anything I *could* say. I got up to leave, but he waved his hand for me to sit down again.

"Perhaps you could stay awhile. I would like to talk. May I offer you a cafe au lait?"

I didn't know what that was, but since it was French, I figured it would be delicious. It turned out to be coffee with a lot of milk in it, for Pete's sake!

He went into the kitchen and turned on a tap. I had never been in his study alone, so I took the opportunity to nose around. There was a picture on his desk of a beautiful dark woman holding a little boy of about three. I guessed that must be his wife. She looked so much younger than M. Lasseur. But maybe that was because I automatically thought of him as old because he was my teacher — my grumpy teacher.

When he came back carrying two steaming cups, I took a good look at him. He wasn't really old at all. I suddenly realized that I had never thought of him as having a life beyond teaching French; I'd never really seen him as a human being.

While we sipped on our drinks, he told me all about his life back in Paris and his dreams of starting a new life here in Canada. I sat and listened to him in fascination as he related one story after another of his student days in France and his marriage to a Jewish girl which caused both families to disown them. He talked for over two hours and I listened, feeling terribly sorry and yet terribly pleased that he had confided in me. Finally he stopped and looked at his watch.

"Oh, my child, it is nearly twelve o'clock! You must forgive me for — what is it you say? — twisting your ear."

I laughed and stood up. "Bending my ear, but you didn't. I loved hearing you talk. It was a wonderful morning."

"For me also, Hope. You have made me forget my pain for a little while." Then he made his face look stern and continued. "Tomorrow we will study the past imperfect. I expect you to have those irregular verbs tightly clasped in your memory. Now, be off and study. I will see you tomorrow."

I left him sitting there in his chair with the picture of his wife and son lying on his knee.

*　　*　　*

The second thing that happened that week involved Jeff, and it was definitely a disaster.

I've already mentioned that Sue Takada was leaving soon to try and get into the armed forces. She was over eighteen and certainly old enough to make up her own mind about how to lead her life. The problem was that she and Jeff had become so close in the short time they had known each other that what Sue did had a terrific impact on Jeff.

It was bad enough when Johnny joined the Air Force and Brian went missing. Jeff seemed to feel it was his responsibility to get in there and do his bit too. But apparently he had decided to wait till he was eighteen — next June — before he made such a drastic move. Until Sue arrived on the scene, that is.

It was Thursday, July 27th, when I came

home from my evening shift at the soda fountain, that I realized what was happening. Lila was in our bedroom still awake and looking mildly annoyed.

"What's the matter?" I asked as soon as I saw her face.

"Oh, nothing really," she sighed. Then a tinge of anger crept into her voice. "It's your brother. I've been waiting for him since eight-thirty. He asked me to drive out to Brockelhurst with him when he came home from work. He said he wanted to talk to me about something, but he hasn't shown up. I know how involved he is with Sue, but I think he could at least have called me."

"Sue leaves tomorrow, doesn't she?" I asked, dropping down on my bed and slipping out of my sandals.

"That's right. I thought maybe that was what he wanted to talk to me about. I was surprised that he didn't want to spend Sue's last night with her, but I supposed she wanted to be with her family."

"And he hasn't gotten in touch with you at all?"

"No, not a word."

I started to feel sick to my stomach. My first inclination was to phone Sue and see if she knew where he was. But it was late and I didn't want to disturb anyone if I could help it. Wordlessly I got up from the bed and went down the hall to Jeff's room. When I went inside I knew immediately what had happened. His dresser was completely bare, and when I checked his drawers I saw that most of his socks and shorts were missing. His closet confirmed my suspicions — his brown suitcase was gone.

I ran out the door and bumped into Lila coming down the hall toward me.

"He's gone, Lila!" I cried.

"Gone? What do you mean? Where did he go?"

"I'm not positive, but I'd bet anything he's taken the bus to Vancouver to enlist. I was afraid this would happen." I ran down the hall to Mom and Dad's room and started pounding on the door.

Dad called a sleepy "Come in," then, as I opened the door, put the light on and muttered, "What on earth's got into you, Hope?"

"It's Jeff," I answered. "He's gone! I think he went off to join the army, or maybe the navy."

Dad was up in a flash and down to Jeff's room, followed by Mom, who stumbled along behind without her glasses on.

"What are we going to do?" she cried, peering

around the room. It was more a plea than a question.

"There's nothing we can do tonight. I'll get on the phone first thing tomorrow and see what I can find out."

"Maybe we could call Sue Takada," I suggested.

"Good idea," Dad agreed. "She might know where he planned to stay."

As it turned out, Sue was as surprised at Jeff's disappearance as we were. They had planned to spend the next day together, then Jeff would take her to the train in the evening. She had no idea where he would be.

After this no-news, we all agreed that there was nothing more to be done tonight and decided to try to get some sleep. Mom said she would phone Aunt Rose in the morning — there was just a chance that Jeff would go there.

"Maybe he went off to stay with one of his friends for the weekend," Dad said hopefully. "He was feeling pretty terrible about Sue leaving; we could be worrying needlessly."

"Sure, that's probably what happened," Lila agreed. Mom and I nodded, but no one was buying the idea.

By noon the next day, we had resigned ourselves to the fact that Jeff was really gone. Lila and I took turns phoning his buddies, but no one knew — or was willing to tell us — where he was. Aunt Rose promised to call the moment he showed up, if he did, and Sue said she would try to get some friends she still knew in Vancouver to locate him.

All I could think was that by the time anyone found him, it might be too late. He could easily get to the recruiting office and be all signed up in a matter of hours. And he did have a head start.

I called Ray, of course, since he was one of Jeff's closest friends, and when he heard what had happened, he drove right into town.

"Try not to worry too much, Hope," he said as he sank into the swing on the front porch. "Jeff's not stupid. He won't do anything without thinking it out very carefully first."

"I'm afraid that's just what he did do," I answered. I sat down beside him and sighed. "Damn this war anyway! Look what it's doing to our family. To everyone's family," I amended, thinking of poor M. Lasseur. "First Brian, then Johnny, now Jeff."

Ray didn't say anything for a moment, then he put his arm around my shoulder. "And me too, if it makes any difference to you," he murmured.

I jumped away from him. "What do you mean?"

"I'm eighteen now, Hope. I can't just sit around doing nothing while every other guy my age is in the war."

"But your dad needs you on the farm!"

"He can get along. I'm joining the R.C.A.F. in the fall."

I didn't say anything for a moment or two. I wondered if he'd be accepted with his missing finger, but I couldn't possibly mention it. I doubted that the Air Force would take anyone who wasn't whole though. I decided to worry about Ray if and when the time came.

"If you think it would be any use, I could catch the train for Vancouver tonight and see if I can find Jeff."

"Oh, Ray, that's terrific of you. But where would you look? We have no idea where he's staying, and Vancouver isn't exactly like Kamloops."

"Yeah, I suppose you're right." He stood up. "I'd better be getting back to the farm now. Call me if you hear anything. And Hope, try not to worry. I'll be here if you need me."

And I knew he would.

Chapter 8
Renovations

On Saturday, July 29th the last big event of that week took place, but it didn't seem to be a disaster at all. In fact, it seemed to be all of my fantasies collected together in glowing technicolour.

I came home from work at about two o'clock, deathly hot and absolutely exhausted, stripped down to my panties and bra and threw myself on the bed. It had been about a hundred and ten in the cafe, and the place was packed the whole time I was on duty. I hadn't been sleeping very well since the night of Jeff's unexpected departure, and all I wanted to do was lie down on the bed and hopefully go into a coma till fall.

Lila was at the desk, writing a letter as usual. She looked up when I came in and smiled. Then, when I started to strip, she got a funny, kind of satisfied look on her face and said, "Come on into the bathroom, Hope. I think it's time you weighed in."

Weighing in was the last thing I wanted to do just then, but I had learned it was best not to argue with Lila. She had a way of making you heel whether you wanted to or not.

I got up and followed her into the bathroom, then dutifully climbed on the scales. While she checked my progress, I closed my eyes and tried to catch a minute or two of sleep. I was just drifting off when her shriek nearly knocked me onto the floor.

"Hope, you made it! Look, one hundred and ten on the nose. You did it!"

I knew I had been losing steadily since that day when I'd tossed back the chocolate bar at McNeil's. I guess Lila hadn't seen me strippe . for a couple of weeks, though, so I could understand why she was so surprised. I turned to the full-length mirror and checked myself out from head to toe. The fat had definitely turned to curves and the skin had cleared up, but I still looked like a shaggy dog. I turned back to Lila and was about to ask her what I could do about the mess on top of my head when she interrupted.

"Okay, now it's time for the renovation." She pulled the laundry hamper into the centre of the room and gestured for me to sit down. "Sit right there until I come back."

104

She returned in a couple of minutes with a pair of scissors, an old sheet, her make-up kit and a Toni Home Permanent. Then she draped the sheet around my neck and started chopping at my hair.

Two hours later I was allowed to look into the mirror. Strangely enough, I wasn't a bit shocked. The fact that I didn't have my glasses on may have had something to do with it, but I merely wondered who the strange brunette with the choirboy hairdo was. I put on my glasses and looked again. She was still there. There wasn't anyone else in the bathroom but Lila, and I knew she was blonde. It had to be me! I started to grin, and saw Lila in the mirror behind me beaming like she had just invented sex.

"I really can't believe it," I sighed as I sat down on the edge of the tub. "How did you do it?"

"I didn't do anything except maybe help nature along a little. You did it all yourself, Hope. I just *knew* there was a Vivien Leigh lurking somewhere under those bangs."

She grabbed my hand and pulled me to my feet.

"It's still early. Let's go down to the park and show you off."

Before I could protest, she had dragged me

into the bedroom and was pulling a white satin bathing suit from her bottom drawer.

"Here, put this on. It's your reward for beating the deadline. You can cover it with one of your broomstick skirts and a blouse until we're ready for your debut."

The suit fit in all the right places, and the skirt actually buttoned up without splitting anywhere. No one was home when we left the house, so we left a note that we would be back in time for supper and headed for the park.

We managed to slip into the women's dressing room without attracting any attention. I shrugged off my skirt and blouse and then stood very still while Lila put a comb through my hair and smoothed my eyebrows.

"There, now you're ready. Come on. We'll go into the soda fountain and knock 'em cold."

"Wait," I said, pulling my glasses off and stuffing them into my beach bag. I looked over to where I thought she should be standing. "Isn't that better?"

"Definitely, but you can't see without your glasses, Hope."

"I know, but you can lead me. Just this once, Lila," I pleaded. "I want to look perfect."

She laughed and I guess nodded her head,

106

because she came over and took my hand. "Just how much can you see anyway?"

"Well, I can sort of make out large buildings. Anything smaller than a piano tends to blur a little."

"Oh, lord! Okay, but just this once. I don't want you running into moving vehicles when I'm not around to guide you."

We left the change room and walked around to the soda fountain.

It really was like a script from one of my more colourful daydreams. In fact, I was a little skeptical at first that it wasn't all just a nice fantasy, and that Anna wouldn't soon be poking me in the ribs and telling me to wake up.

But it was real, all right.

There was the usual group of seniors taking over the back three tables of the big open room. The younger kids were sitting at the counter, and they were the first to notice us.

One of them called out to Lila, which caused the seniors to perk up. She was still a very big attraction. A couple of the older boys got up and came to meet us.

"Hey, Lila, come on back and join us," one of them invited.

"And bring your friend," his buddy added eagerly.

I couldn't believe it. I had known those two since I was in training pants, and they didn't recognize me. Of course, they were Jeff's friends and probably hadn't ever really looked at me — the pesky kid sister.

Meanwhile the kids at the counter and the front booths were starting to buzz.

"Who's the cute girl with Hope's cousin?"

"Is she new in town?"

"I wonder if she's related to Hope Mather?"

The next thing I knew we were being herded to the back and eased into chairs. Finally someone broke the ice.

"Okay, Lila, who's your friend?"

I kind of squinted for a second to see if I could focus on the faces around the table. As far as I could make out, they were all friends of Jeff who had been at our house off and on for about ten years. I couldn't see Troy Farnham among them, which was a bit of a disappointment.

Lila was struggling to keep from laughing and not succeeding too well.

"This is my cousin, Hope Mather," she answered, choking on the words. "I thought you all knew her."

108

"This is Hope Mather? Jeff's little sister? The one who looks like a Brussels sprout?"

"Where have you been hiding her?"

"You're not telling me this is that funny looking little fat kid with all the hair?"

That's just a sample of the complimentary remarks that came pouring out. I think Lila enjoyed the whole thing almost as much as I did. She probably felt like that Pygmalion guy we read about last year in English Lit.

Somebody ordered cherry cokes for us, and everyone started talking to me at once. Being the centre of attention was almost too much for me. I didn't know what to say or do. It was real heady stuff, all right, but at the same time sort of scary. I guess Lila saw my discomfort and decided she'd better rescue me before I panicked.

"We've got to get home," she announced, downing the last of her drink. "Dinner is in half an hour." She stood up and reached for my hand.

At this point, three guys all tried to get out of the booth at the same time.

"I've got my car just up the hill," one said. "I'd be glad to drive you home."

"No point in you ladies walking all that way in this heat when my *convertible* is just across the park," the second countered.

The third just stood staring at me while an overturned bottle of Pepsi ran over the table and onto his feet.

"No, thank you," Lila said. "We're going to take a quick dip, then walk home. We need the exercise."

She turned and strolled down the aisle, holding me by the hand so I wouldn't wipe out any chairs or tables on the way.

As we swept past the kids at the counter, I could hear two very familiar voices in the crowd behind us.

"Shirley, do you see who I see?"

"Where? Oh, you mean that pretty girl with Lila. I wonder if she's related — Oh, my God! It can't be!"

"It is, though. I knew she was losing weight, but just look at her. She looks like Gene Tierney."

"Boy, that does it. If Hope can get down to that size, so can I!"

Anna laughed. "Then maybe you'd better leave the rest of that chocolate sundae."

"Waste not, want not. I'll start tomorrow."

Oh, how familiar *that* refrain was!

* * *

When we got home, Mom and Dad were in the

dining room setting the table. At least, Mom was; Dad was sitting there watching her. They seemed to not want to be out of each other's sight ever since Jeff left.

Their reaction, when they saw us in the door-way, was everything I could have hoped for.

Dad whistled and Mom turned around to see what he was looking at. She peered near-sight-edly at me, took off her glasses, cleaned them on a napkin and peered again.

I still had my wet bathing suit on under my clothes, so I quickly slipped off my skirt and blouse and struck an exaggerated model's pose.

Mom was the first to speak.

"Hope, dear, you look absolutely stunning. Your complexion has completely cleared up and that extra weight . . . I knew you were getting thinner, of course, but I couldn't really tell how much you'd lost under the baggy clothes."

"Is this really my little dumpling?" Dad came over and turned me around. "I never would have believed it."

"I hope you don't mind that I cut her hair," Lila said.

"Mind? I've been trying to get her to come out from under that bush for years!" Mom smiled at me like she had just given birth to Elizabeth Taylor, then her face crumpled.

"If only Jeff could see you," she sniffed. "He would be so proud."

Dad cleared his throat and muttered, "Better get out of those wet suits before you catch your death of cold."

It was still in the low nineties, but Dad was never known to be terribly subtle.

When we came back downstairs, Mom had dinner on the table and her emotions under control.

"Wait till Ray sees you," she exclaimed, automatically handing the potato salad past me to Lila and offering me the carrot sticks. "He'll be bowled over."

"You've got a date with him tonight, haven't you?" Lila asked.

"Yep. He's coming at seven." I looked at my watch. "Holy Toledo, it's six-thirty already!" I grabbed a couple of slices of cold chicken and jumped up from the table. "Sorry, but I've got to get ready, and I need to phone Anna before Ray gets here."

No one gave me any static about leaving the table halfway through dinner. A date with Ray gave me the freedom to do practically anything.

They all thought he was Bing Crosby and President Roosevelt rolled into one. As for phoning Anna, they never stopped that. There was always the chance she had heard from Sue and had news of Jeff.

Anna answered on the first ring. Shirley had gone to her place for dinner, and they were just getting ready to call me. Before I could get a word in, the two of them were talking into the receiver at once.

"Hope, what did you do to yourself?"

"I could hardly believe my eyes."

"Was it hard to diet? Did you have to practically live on lettuce?"

"Your hair is so cute. And your eyes looked so blue. I never really noticed them before."

I laughed happily. "Yes, it was hard to diet, and no, I didn't have to live on lettuce. I was allowed the odd radish or carrot stick. As for the hair, Lila gave me one of those new home perms."

"But what did you do to your eyes?"

"Just a little mascara and eyebrow pencil. Lila's a real artist."

"You can say that again!" Shirley cried. She could have been a bit more tactful, I thought, but then she was probably a little envious. I know I would have been if our roles had been reversed.

"Look, I've got a date with Ray and I'm late, but I just had to hear what you two would say."

"All I've got to say is, you looked sensational," Anna answered. "I really didn't recognize you at first."

"Me either," Shirley agreed. "You've given me inspiration, Hope. I'm going to lose twenty-five pounds. If you can do it, so can I."

"Good for you," I replied. "I'll call you tomorrow." I hung up the phone and ran humming upstairs to fix my face.

It was when I was redoing my eyes that I realized I had totally forgotten to ask Anna if she had heard anything from Sue.

Ray's reaction to my altered appearance was definitely underwhelming. When I came downstairs, he had already arrived and was sitting at the dining room table with the family, eating strawberry shortcake. He looked up when I came into the room and smiled.

"Hey, Hope, you've done something to your hair. It's pretty. Well, maybe just a little." I assumed this last remark was in answer to Mom's offer of more cake and not a qualification of my prettiness, although I wouldn't have bet on it.

I guess Lila must have seen my expression,

because she started to laugh so hard that she had to excuse herself from the table. Even Mom was having a hard time not smiling. Only Dad didn't notice.

"Hasn't my little pumpkin blossomed overnight, Ray? Doesn't she look great?"

Ray looked up from his shortcake with a puzzled expression.

"Well, yes, I guess so," he answered very unconvincingly. He looked over to where I was standing, waiting for the cries of admiration I expected to hear, and smiled again.

"She always looks great as far as I'm concerned," he answered, then turned his attention back to spearing the last strawberry on his plate.

I was beginning to wonder if maybe he really *did* think pregnant sows were beautiful.

The reaction of the gang at the Top Hat, where we went after the show, was much more rewarding, however. I persuaded Ray to take me there for a coke, and I guess he realized that I wanted people to see my new look, because he didn't argue at all. I purposely dawdled on the way so we could make an entrance with the place full.

Word had apparently got out that Hope Mather had turned into a girl, and when we walked in all heads turned to look at us. I suddenly realized I had my ugly glasses on. Pretending to drop my purse, I bent over and slipped them into my pocket. The room of astonished faces immediately became a blur. I took Ray's hand so I wouldn't fall on anyone as he led me to a booth just past the counter.

We ordered our drinks to the background buzz of low conversation. It was very satisfying to know I was its subject. Ray seemed to be quite oblivious to the stir we were making; at least, he pretended to be. I guess he understood just how much this whole thing meant to me though, because his smile was very knowing when he asked, "What happened to your glasses, Hope? Did the movie bother your eyes?"

"Ah . . . yes," I answered. "My glasses sometimes irritate them when I've been in the dark for a long time." I realize it was pathetic, but it was the only thing I could think of on the spur of the moment. I felt a little silly, but the next minute I was thanking my lucky stars that I had removed them.

"Hi, Ray," a voice was saying somewhere above me. "Mind if we join you?"

I couldn't see the face that far away, but I certainly recognized the voice.

"Yeah, okay," was Ray's reluctant reply, and the next thing I knew Troy Farnham was sliding into the booth next to me.

"Well, aren't you going to introduce us, Ray?" Troy asked after a moment's silence. "Or don't you want to share her?"

The booth was narrow enough that I could see Ray's expression. It wasn't pleasant. Neither was the expression on Laurie McVale's face. She looked as if she would like to set fire to my underwear. Troy didn't seem to notice.

"Troy Farnham — Hope Mather. You know Laurie, of course."

"This is Hope Mather?" Laurie's fire engine voice ricocheted around the room. "Good lord, what have you done to yourself?"

I could feel everyone's eyes on me and my face began to heat up.

"Can it, Laurie," Troy ordered. Then to me, "Of course, you're the little girl at McNeil's. The one with the great throwing arm." He laughed and I got hotter.

"What does he mean by that, Hope?" Ray sounded almost belligerent.

"I threw a milk shake at him," I answered, wishing that a nice quiet bomb would fall.

"Oh, God, that sounds like you, Hope," Laurie groaned.

Troy ignored her and turned to me. "We were on our way out to the lake. Would you guys like to come along?"

"That would be — " I didn't get any further before Ray interrupted.

"Sorry, but I have to get up early tomorrow. A lot of work to do around the farm. Maybe some other time. Come on, Hope, let's go."

I knew he didn't work on Sundays this time of year, but I didn't make a big thing of it. Troy made some remark about nine-thirty not being exactly the witching hour, but when Ray glared at him, he stood up for me to slide past.

Troy's last words as he sat down again across from Laurie were, "I'll take a raincheck then." And he winked at me.

I gave him my best smile — the one I used to practise for hours in front of the mirror — and said something about looking forward to it.

Ray had me by the hand and out the door before Troy could answer.

Chapter 9
Deception

Troy called the next day.

"Hi. Is that you, Hope? It's Troy Farnham."

"Yes, I know. I'll get Lila."

"No. It's you I want to talk to. I was wondering if you'd like to go for a little drive. Maybe stop some place for supper."

I looked at the hall clock: three-thirty. Dinner was at five. Ray hadn't been at church that morning, but he had called later and Mom had suggested that he come in for dinner as usual. He would be arriving in an hour at the latest. There was no way I could go for even a short drive and get back in time. My big chance and I had to turn it down!

"Gee, I'm sorry, Troy, but I just can't. We're having company for dinner and I have to help get it ready."

"Okay. Maybe another time."

"Oh, yes. That would be super." I hoped I didn't sound as desperate as I felt.

"I have to go out of town tomorrow for a few days. I'll call you when I get back."

Before I could answer, the receiver clicked in my ear.

"Who was that on the phone?" Mom asked as I strolled into the kitchen, still in a mild fog.

She and Lila were at the table shelling peas. They both looked up inquiringly as I came in. I tried to play it real casual as I sat down across from them, but it didn't come off. I was so nervous from the phone call that I knocked the bowl on the floor.

"No one," I answered, getting down on my knees and chasing after the scattered peas. "Just a friend."

When I came up, they were both looking at me strangely, especially Lila. I tried to remember if I had mentioned Troy's name. I was afraid maybe I had.

For some reason I didn't want Lila to know Troy had called. Maybe it was because she had dated him first, or maybe I felt guilty about Ray. At any rate, I didn't want to stick around and have to explain, so I excused myself and went up to my room. I lay on my bed, thinking of Troy and the incredible possibility that he might actually want to take me out, until Mom called that Ray had arrived.

The rest of the day and evening went by without me. I tried to keep up my end of the conversation, but a reasonably intelligent grunt was about the best I could manage. Ray left earlier than usual, which was okay by me, and Lila started quizzing me, which wasn't. I managed to fend off her concerned questions about my behaviour by pleading uncontrollable fatigue, and escaped upstairs and into bed without even washing my face. When she came in a little later, I pretended to be fast asleep.

*　　*　　*

Troy's call was just the beginning. I started getting asked out by boys who didn't know I was alive the week before. It was just like one of those grade B college movies where the ugly duckling suddenly becomes the most popular kid on the block. I didn't accept any of the offers, mostly because I had to work every night, but that didn't stop some of the more persistent ones. They started coming into McNeil's and hanging around talking to me. Gerry wasn't exactly thrilled with the whole scene since they took up stool space and spent about ten cents per night. It was great for me though. I started being able to talk back without going into cardiac arrest, and by the end of the week I was really getting the hang of the ancient art of flirting.

I guess that week should have been about the most perfect of my entire life, and at the time I thought it was. I had everything I had ever wanted: good looks, boys flocking around me, self-confidence. I spent a lot of time experimenting with make-up and shopping for clothes. The only problem was that it didn't leave me much time for Lila and our cozy chats, or for Shirley and Anna either.

By the time Saturday rolled around, the phone calls had dropped off and so had the customers. I still had lots of offers to date, but I guess the novelty of Hope Mather, glamour girl, was wearing a bit thin. That depressed me more than I cared to admit. Then, to add to my gloom, when I came into work at noon Gerry handed me a letter.

"This came for you this morning," he grunted. "I don't know why anyone would write to you here."

Puzzled, I took the envelope and glanced at the handwriting. Immediately I knew why it was addressed to me here and not at the house. It was from Jeff.

I tore it open and my eyes flew over the page. I was reading so fast that I wasn't understanding a word, so I made myself calm down and start again from the beginning.

Dear Hopeless,

You're probably wondering why I'm writing to you instead of Mom and Dad and why I addressed the letter to Gerry's. Well, it's because I need a favour from you.

First, let me tell you I'm okay so you can stop worrying about me — that is, if you were worrying. Ha, ha. I'm just fine. I'm staying with a friend of Brian's I met when we were here a couple of years ago. He told me if I ever came to Vancouver to look him up, so I did. Now please don't tell the folks where I am. They'll only come rushing out here and drag me back home.

What I want you to do is get my birth certificate and send it to me. Mom keeps all that kind of stuff in the bottom drawer of her bureau under a bunch of photo albums, in case you didn't know. The thing is, I can't get into the Air Force without it. Yeah, I know it proves I'm only seventeen, but there's a guy I met here who, for a slight fee, can alter it so not even an expert can catch the change.

I suppose you think I'm crazy trying to enlist, but I just can't stand the idea of Sue going off to try and get into the army and me having to stay home and rot in a schoolroom for another year. I hope you'll understand.

I'm counting on you, Hopeless. When you get it, send it to the above address. DON'T LET ME DOWN!

Love, Jeff

I read it over two more times, and it didn't get a bit better. My first impulse was to go out to Vancouver and punch Jeff's teeth down his throat for putting me in this horrible position. My second was to go out to Vancouver and put my arms around him. I thought I knew what he was going through and I was crying inside for him.

Since neither impulse was practical, I stuffed the letter in the pocket of my apron and went to work. I would decide what to do later.

I guess my mind was still on Jeff and whether I should tell the folks I'd heard from him. Otherwise, I would have noticed right away when Troy came in.

When I did see him, he was seated at the counter studying the menu. His head was bent, which gave me a chance to dash into the back and check the mirror. I redid my make-up, combed my hair, then after hesitating a moment, took off my glasses and stuffed them in my apron pocket.

He looked up when I came over to him and smiled at me.

"Hi there. I was hoping I'd find you here," he said as I stood waiting to take his order.

Suddenly all the cool I had developed over the past week left me and I reverted to the overweight live nerve I had been the first time he spoke to me. First I dropped my pencil. Then I banged my nose on the counter as I bent down to grope for it. My nose started to bleed, so I hunched down under the counter and tried to stop it. When I finally surfaced, Troy was bending over the counter to see what was the matter, and I hit him under the chin with my head. I think he would have been happier if I'd just thrown another milk shake at him.

"Look, you're pretty busy right now. Why don't I come back later and drive you home?"

The place was filling up and Gerry was doing a lot of throat clearing behind me.

"I'd like that," I managed to mumble. "I'm through at one-thirty."

"Fine," he answered. "I'll be waiting outside for you."

I wouldn't have been a bit surprised if he had changed his mind about taking me home as soon as he was out the door. Maybe I didn't look like a spotty watermelon any more, but who would want to be seen with an uncoordinated retardate? I put on my glasses and finished my shift, miserable but sighted. I wanted nothing more than to go home and jump into a warm bath in which, if my luck held, I would quietly drown.

But when I went out onto the street an hour later, there was Troy sitting in his car across the street waiting for me. As I started across the street with my glasses still on — I wasn't ready to risk sudden traffic death for beauty just yet — he got out of the car and went around to open the passenger door.

When he had closed it behind me and was walking back to his side, I suddenly remembered the glasses and slipped them off, but not before he had seen them.

"I'd forgotten you wore specs," he said. "They sure make you look different."

126

"I only wear them to read small print," I lied, tucking them into my purse.

"That's good. I hate glasses." He put the car in gear, and we roared up Second Street in silence.

When we arrived at the house, Troy turned to me and said, "How about taking that drive tonight. I thought we might go out to Tranquille, then stop for a drink when it gets a little cooler."

"That sounds like a wonderful idea," I answered, surprised at how controlled I managed to sound.

"Good. I'll pick you up about eight." He got out and came around to open the door for me. Then he took my hand and walked me up to the front porch. Not only did he make me feel like Princess Elizabeth, but he probably saved me from falling headfirst into the honeysuckle bush at the side of the path. I could barely make out the house, let alone incidentals like large hedges.

As he reached around me to open the front door, he brushed his lips across my forehead and whispered, "I can't wait till tonight." Beyond speech, I nodded and quietly floated into the house and up to our bedroom.

Lila wasn't anywhere in sight, so I threw myself onto the bed and began to go over every

127

second of the past couple of hours. I'd made a fool of myself at the cafe, but Troy didn't seem to mind. He had actually asked me for a date, and my biggest fantasy was going to come true — I'd walk into the Top Hat on Saturday night with Troy Farnham.

Saturday night! I suddenly realized I had a date with Ray that night. What was I going to do? I couldn't possibly turn Troy down a second time, he'd never ask me again. Besides, I didn't know for sure how to get hold of him. I really had no choice.

I ran into the hall, gave the operator Ray's number, and prayed no one could hear me from downstairs.

"Ray? It's me, Hope," I said when the phone was answered. "Look, I'm awfully sorry, but I'm feeling just terrible. I think it might be summer flu. So I'm afraid I won't be able to go to the show with you tonight."

"Gee, I'm sorry, Hope. But if you're feeling rotten you'd better get right to bed. You've got to be in good shape for the barn dance next Saturday."

"Barn — Oh, sure. Yes, well, I'll be okay in a day or two. I'm really sorry, but you know how it is."

128

"Sure, Hope. You take care now."

"Right," I said, and hung up feeling crumbier than I wanted to admit. But, on the other hand, I wasn't really hurting Ray. The chances of him being in the Top Hat that night were about one in a million, so he would never need to know. And I'd make it up to him somehow, I promised myself.

As I turned to walk back to the room, Lila came up the stairs. I ran to meet her and started to throw my arms around her. She sort of shrugged me off and moved on to the bedroom.

"Lila, what's the matter?" I asked, following her into the room.

She sat down on the bed and looked up at me.

"I saw you drive up with Troy Farnham. Hope, please don't get involved with him. He's not for you."

"I'm sorry, Lila, but I think he's the greatest thing since nylon stockings, and until today just about as difficult for me to get."

"Troy isn't very hard to get, believe me. He'll come on to anything in skirts, provided she's good-looking enough for him to be seen with."

I started to get angry. How did she know what Troy was really like? She'd only gone out with him once. He'd apparently never asked her again, so now she was bad-mouthing him. I decided to drop the matter and walked out of the room.

Lila, however, was not ready to drop it. She followed me down the hall to the bathroom and sat on the edge of the tub as I started to strip for my bath.

"Ray is a really great guy, Hope. Don't spoil things with him for someone like Troy."

I felt a nasty stab of guilt as I thought of my phone call to Ray. My face must have showed it, because Lila came on even stronger.

"Any girl would be lucky to date Ray even once, and you've been practically going steady. He may not be as good-looking as Troy, but he's got more character in his little finger than Troy has in his whole bronzed body."

I started to giggle. "Which little finger?" I asked.

"That's not funny, Hope. Surely you must realize by now how unimportant looks are. Ray sure does."

"Yeah, I guess I do," I nodded, knowing that I was lying through my teeth. Looks were everything. Hadn't I proved it personally?

"You've got a date with him tonight, haven't you?" She really knew how to put in the spurs.

130

"I did have, but he cancelled. He's not feeling well." At least I was consistent in my lies.

"Too bad. Want to go to the movies with me? I'm dateless too," she smiled.

"Actually, Lila, I'm going out with Troy. It's not a real date," I added guiltily. "He's just taking me for a little drive."

"I see." The smile disappeared. "Hope, I really don't think that's a good idea. You don't know — "

"Look, Lila, it's okay. I know what I'm doing and I'm not going to let you talk me out of it. It's my life, you know."

She sighed and nodded. Neither of us said anything as she walked out of the room and shut the door.

When I finished my bath, I went back to the bedroom and lay down. I guess I must have been more tired than I thought because I fell into a deep sleep. I awoke some time later to Mom calling me to come down to dinner. I couldn't believe it — it was after six o'clock already!

I got up and ran downstairs just as Mom and Dad and Lila were sitting down at the table. Lila didn't look at me, although I tried to catch her eye and smile. Mom didn't seem to notice the frigid air that was flowing between us though, and pretty soon she was off on her favourite topic.

"I can't understand why Jeff hasn't written. He must know how worried we all are."

My fork clattered onto my plate and my hair started to rise on the back of my neck. I'd forgotten all about the letter from Jeff and the decision I was going to have to make. Dad must have noticed my expert imitation of sheer terror.

"What's the matter, Hope? You look like you've just put your finger in a live socket."

"It's nothing," I answered, and tried to look less stunned. "I just thought of something I'm supposed to do for French." My lying was getting positively professional. "If you'll excuse me, I'm not very hungry." I got up and rushed out of the room before anyone could object.

My purse was lying on my bed where I had thrown it when I came in from work. I opened it and reached inside for Jeff's letter. I couldn't feel it, so I dumped everything onto the bed, then looked down in disbelief. It wasn't there! I tried to remember what I had done with it after I had read it, and realized that I had put it in my apron pocket. It must still be there. I breathed a sigh of relief. No need to worry about it or about Jeff's request. There wasn't a thing I could do till Monday. Meanwhile, I had to decide what I was going to wear for my date.

When I came back downstairs, the family had finished dinner and were all sitting in the living room listening to "Your Hit Parade." When Mom saw how I was dressed, she asked me where I was going. I told her and she said, "I don't think I know him, do I?"

"No, Mom. He's Mrs. Ellis's nephew. He's just here for the summer."

"I see. How old is he, Hope?"

"I don't really know. About eighteen, I guess."

"Too old," Dad announced from behind the paper.

"But, Dad, you let me go out with Raymond Rounds, and he's eighteen."

Mom looked from one of us to the other. She's always trusted me and has never put any big restrictions on my social life, except the time I have to be home. She obviously didn't know what to say, so she turned to Lila.

"What do you think? Is this Troy person reliable?"

Lila looked at me, then at Mom. She tightened her lips and shook her head. "I don't think it's any of my business, Aunt Prue."

I was holding my breath. Mom looked at Dad, who shrugged and said, "It's up to you, dear."

Finally she gave a slight nod of her head. "Well, since you've already accepted, I guess it will be all right this time. But remember, be home by eleven."

A horn began honking outside the house. I ran to the window and saw Troy standing beside the car gesturing to me. He obviously didn't want to have to run across Lila.

"Thanks, Mom," I cried, and grabbed my purse as I headed for the door.

"Doesn't that young man have enough manners to come up to the house?" Dad grumbled. "I don't think — "

Before he could let me know what it was he didn't think, I was out the door. I pulled my glasses off and jammed them in my purse, then groped my way carefully down the path to the car.

"You look sensational, Hope," Troy greeted me as he helped me into the car.

He slipped in beside me and I could see he was wearing white duck pants and a green shirt opened to the waist. He looked good enough to eat.

There was no doubt about it — we made a great-looking couple.

Chapter 10
Hated by all

As we drove away from the house, I began to panic. What would I talk about? It was so important to make a good impression; I had to sound cool but interesting. Sure, and just exactly how would I do that?

As it turned out, I didn't need to worry. Troy took over the conversational ball and carried it until we drove into the sanitarium grounds. Tranquille is a place for people with tuberculosis. It has a lot of buildings and houses scattered over a vast park-like area. The public is allowed to use the grounds as long as they don't try to go into any of the buildings without permission. As we drove down toward the river, Troy finished telling me about his plans to go to the University of British Columbia that fall.

"I wanted to join up but they wouldn't take me," he explained as he manoeuvered the car into a sheltered spot out of sight of any of the buildings. "I have a slight heart murmur."

"Oh, that's terrible!" I exclaimed.

"Not really. It doesn't bother me that much. I just wish I could be doing my part for my country instead of wasting my time at school. Although I'm sure it'll be good fun." He killed the engine and put his arm around my shoulder. "There'll be lots of parties, and the fraternity I plan to pledge is the best on campus. Too bad you can't be there, Hope. That would make it perfect." He took my chin in his hand and turned my face toward his. "But we still have the rest of the summer," he added, and kissed me right on the mouth.

I won't go into details about the next half hour. I only know that the last time I felt that way was when I got my first two-wheeler. By the time he drew away and suggested we get back to town, I was about as controlled as a bowl of tapioca.

Neither of us spoke until we crossed the North Kamloops bridge and were heading up Victoria street.

"McNeil's or the Top Hat?" Troy asked.

"Top Hat," I replied, figuring we'd be seen by more people there than at McNeil's on a Saturday night. Besides, Gerry knows Ray pretty well and he just might say something to him about seeing me with Troy.

The place was packed as usual. The show had

137

just got out and everyone was there. We walked past the counter and found a booth in the back with another couple in it. They squeezed together so we could fit in on either side, and Troy introduced me. Their names were Jake and Jennie Something; I didn't catch the last name and was too shy to ask Troy to repeat it. They apparently came from Troy's home town and had come back with him to visit for a week or so. They looked like they were quite a bit older than Troy, probably in their twenties, and were talking about a party they were planning sometime the next week. The gist of the conversation was where they would get enough ration coupons for the booze.

I started to panic a little, wondering what I would do if Troy asked me to the party. One of the few rules my parents laid down was that I couldn't go anywhere there was drinking. I decided to worry about it if he really did ask me though, and sat back to enjoy myself.

I have no idea who was in the cafe other than the people at our table. Everyone else was a big blur. I tried to hear the conversation around me and perhaps recognize voices, but it was useless. There were too many people all talking at once for me to zero in on any one voice.

The conversation about the party finished

and Troy brought out a package of Sweet Caps. He took one, then offered the package to me, and although I've never been into smoking, I felt I had to take one. It was as bad as Mom and Dad always told me it would be, but I puffed valiantly and managed to fake my way through the whole cigarette without coughing more than once. While I was fighting asphyxiation, Troy and the other couple began commenting on the people around us.

It was pretty innocuous, mostly remarks about someone's clothes or the way they wore their hair, until Troy suddenly sat up straight and looked past me to the door.

"Well, well," he announced in a voice that cut through the hubbub like a well-aimed paper airplane. "Look who's just come in — Mr. Moto and his friends."

I turned, but couldn't see anything beyond the side of the booth.

A group of people came toward us and Anna's voice said, "Hi, Hope. How are you doing?"

I looked up and could just make out Anna and Shirley standing beside Lyle Takada and Billy Gee, Anna's boyfriend.

"Hi," I answered, feeling vaguely uncomfortable. I was about to introduce them to Troy and the other couple when Troy began talking to Jake

139

about fishing and completely ignored me. Anna gave me a half smile and the group moved on.

"I had no idea you were friendly with the enemy, Hope," Troy said when they were out of my limited range of vision. "Got any German buddies as well?"

I laughed uncomfortably and tried to change the subject, but Troy wasn't having any of it.

"Those people shouldn't be allowed to come into public places where good Canadians are. They pollute the air. Don't you agree, Hope?"

I thought he was joking and answered, "Oh, definitely. We can't have the yellow peril lurking around listening to our secrets, can we?"

Jake and Jennie laughed, but Troy looked dead serious. "That's for damn sure," he nodded.

I couldn't believe it. Was he really that bigoted? I began to wonder if it was possible he might have a flaw. Then he smiled and put his arm around me, saying, "It's getting late, honey. I don't want your folks to ground you on account of breaking curfew. Come on, I'll take you home," and I instantly abandoned any idea that he wasn't perfection personified.

It was just short of eleven when we drove up in front of our house. I would have been happy to take my chances and go in late, but Troy was out of the car and around to my door before I could speak. He took my hand and led me up the path, just like that afternoon, and when we got to the porch I asked him if he'd like to come in for a coke or something.

"Not tonight," he answered. "Maybe another time. I'll call you." He bent over, kissed me quickly and was gone.

I was a little disturbed by his obvious hurry to get away, but consoled myself with his promise that he would call. I went into the house and up to bed in a state of delirious excitement. And confusion.

*   *   *

The next day, Sunday, was about as bad as Saturday was good.

Lila was up and downstairs when I woke up, so I didn't know whether she was still put out with me or not. I decided maybe I would leave her alone for a while to get over it and spend the day with Anna and Shirley.

I went down the hall to the upstairs extension and gave the operator Shirley's number. I would see if she wanted to go swimming.

"Oh, it's you," was her less-than-enthusiastic reply to my call. "What do you want?"

"To see if you want to go to the park this afternoon." I wanted to talk about my incredible experience with my first real kiss, but decided it might be better not to mention it right now. She was sounding downright hostile.

"Oh, really? I'm surprised you'd still want to be seen with us."

"What are you talking about?"

"I'm sure you know, Hope. But please don't expect me, or Anna either, to be as impressed with you as you seem to be."

I didn't say anything for a moment. I wasn't sure what *to* say.

"Are we going to the park together or not?" I finally broke the silence.

"Anna and I are. I don't know about you."

This conversation was not going at all the way I'd hoped.

"Well, if you don't want me, just say so. There are plenty of other people around, you know."

"Fine, I don't. Maybe you can get your precious Troy Farnham to go with you. I'm sure he'd welcome the opportunity to show all the poor dull little Kamloops girls his beautiful muscles." I didn't get a chance to reply. She hung up the phone.

I sat there with the dead receiver in my hand until the operator came on and demanded, "Number, please." I gave her Anna's number and was told the line was busy. Shirley, no doubt, gloating about telling me off.

And I hadn't the remotest idea why.

I wandered out onto the porch and sat down on the swing. What had gotten into Shirley anyway? Then it hit me. She had seen me with Troy last night and was jealous! She was a really super kid, but she definitely didn't set the town on fire with her looks. She and I had always been a pair — the school blimps. Now I'd changed, and she was left to carry the banner alone. I felt sad for her, but I couldn't help but be secretly pleased. After fifteen years, somebody actually envied me.

To heck with all of them! I thought. I didn't need anyone. I could always go to the park by myself. I jumped up from the swing and went to bathe and dress.

In the bathroom I slipped my pyjamas off, and stepping on the scales, discovered I'd got rid of another pound. I stopped to admire my new figure again in the mirror and checked my skin for any signs of blemishes. It was as clear as a two-year-old's. I had just started running the tub when I heard the phone ring. I grabbed a towel and draped it around me as I ran for the upstairs extension. Maybe it was Troy. But Lila got there before me. I was just in time to hear her say, "Oh, hi, Ray. How are you feeling?"

Suddenly it was very hot in the hall. I could feel the perspiration trickling down my back as I watched Lila listening to whatever Ray was saying. Her voice when she finally spoke was low and angry.

"She's just fine now, Ray. She's in the bath so she can't come to the phone, but I'll tell her you called."

I slipped back through the door and closed it silently behind me. Lila had found out I'd lied about Ray being sick, and what was worse, that I'd lied to Ray about me. I didn't look forward to seeing her. I wondered how long I could reasonably stay in the bathroom and decided that all day was asking a bit much. I'd have to come out some time, and Lila would be waiting to pounce on me.

I turned the taps off and stepped into the tub. As I lay back and let the water flow around me, I thought of the night before in Troy's car. Pretty soon Lila and everyone else had faded into the wallpaper.

*   *   *

"Your dress looks absolutely fabulous," Lila was saying as she adjusted my tiara. "You and Troy will make an incredible King and Queen of the Arts Ball."

I looked at myself in the mirror in her bedroom. I did look great. The pink strapless chiffon gown was tight across the bodice and down to the hips, where it fell away into yards of billowing gathers. I wore a single strand of pearls that Troy had given me just that afternoon.

"For the most beautiful girl on campus," he had whispered as he fastened them around my neck. "You make all the other co-eds look like Lassie."

I knew I was good-looking; everyone told me so. But to be chosen Queen of the Arts Ball was an honour no freshman had ever had. I thought at first that Troy had had something to do with it, but I was told later that I was voted in on my own merit.

"Here, wear my fur jacket," Lila was saying as a loud rapping began at the front door. It must be Troy. The rapping continued louder and was followed by —

*   *   *

"For heaven's sake, Hope, are you planning to stay in there for the duration?" Dad's voice bellowed. "There are others of us who would like to leave the house clean too."

I sat up in the cold water and shivered. I couldn't put it off any longer. I'd have to leave the lovely safety of the bathroom and go into the bed-room where Lila was sure to be waiting. Sud-denly I wanted a chocolate brownie more than life itself.

Lila was lying on her bed with her eyes closed when I came into the room. She didn't open them and I hoped for a moment that she was asleep. That dream died quickly as she spoke.

"I know it's none of my business, Hope, but Ray is a really great guy and I don't like to see him hurt. Even more important, I don't want to see you get hurt, and you're bound to if you start running around with Troy Farnham and his crowd."

I decided maybe the best defense would be an offense.

"Look, Lila, I didn't ask Raymond Rounds to chase me. It was his idea. I never agreed to go steady or anything, so what do I owe him?"

"Don't you think you owe him the truth? If you didn't want to go out with him, why didn't you just tell him so instead of making up some story about having the flu?"

"I didn't want to hurt his feelings," I mut-tered. "And thanks for not giving me away."

"I did it for Ray, not you." Her voice softened as she continued. "Please listen to me, Hope. I know what kind of stuff goes on at Troy's parties and what he expects of his girls. Keep away from him. He's bad news."

"Are you sure you don't want me to keep away from him so you'll have a clear shot at him yourself?" The moment I said it I was sorry. But it was out and echoing from the walls of the room.

"My God! I've created a monster!" Lila cried as she sat up and threw her legs over the sides of the bed. "If I could, I'd put all those pounds and that hair right back on. You were a lot nicer when you were fat and funny-looking!" She stood up and flounced out of the room.

"Please, Lila, I didn't mean that," I called, but she either didn't hear me or pretended not to.

Now I'd really done it. What a stupid thing to say! I knew Lila didn't care about anyone but Johnny, but I was getting pretty fed up with her constant criticism of Troy. She hadn't given him a chance. I sat on the bed staring into space until both the guilt and anger I had been feeling disappeared.

Well, I certainly wasn't going to let Lila or anyone else spoil my day. I'd go to the park alone, and the way I looked now, I was pretty sure I wouldn't be alone long.

But I was.

None of the seniors, including Troy, were anywhere in sight. In fact, there weren't many kids there at all — kids my age, that is. There were hundreds of little kids, screaming and throwing balls and stepping on the faces of anyone who was foolish enough to be lying down trying to tan. It was very obviously family day at the park. Old men in their forties had got up a baseball game, and their equally ancient wives were sitting under the trees gossiping and knitting khaki garments.

Shirley and Anna were out on the raft where they were relatively safe from the grade school set. I wanted to swim out and join them, but when I called out to them, they pretended not to hear. So I swam out and back without stopping, then went in and changed back to my skirt and halter. There was no point in sticking around any longer — I'd wasted practically the whole day already. I might just as well go home and work on my French.

I started the long climb up the hill to the house feeling let down and hurt. I wondered where Troy was and who he was with. Then I started to think about Raymond. I wished I hadn't lied to him. He was a good friend. Lila was right — he deserved better. Lila. She'd probably never want to have anything more to do with me. She and Shirley and Anna.

But there was always tomorrow. Troy had

said he would call. Suddenly everything started to look a lot better. I'd make up with Lila; I'd call Ray; Shirley and Anna would soon come around. Even though it was over ninety-five degrees, I ran the rest of the way home singing "The Boogie Woogie Bugle Boy from Company B" at the top of my lungs.

The fates, however, were not going to let me get off that easily.

When I opened the front door, I knew there was something the matter. Mom and Dad were sitting in the living room as usual on a Sunday evening, but they weren't listening to Charlie McCarthy. Only major floods and minor earthquakes could keep them from listening to their favourite radio programme, and I hadn't noticed either occurring in the neighbourhood. I had a ghastly premonition it might have something to do with me.

I tried to slip upstairs without them seeing me, but it was no good.

"Hope, come in here, please." Dad's voice didn't leave any room for argument.

I poked my head in the entranceway and saw they were sitting together on the chesterfield. An envelope lay between them. I walked slowly over to a chair beside them and sat down.

"When did you receive this letter, Hope?" Mom asked, handing me the envelope.

I started to take it, puzzled at her sharp manner, then as I glanced down, my eye caught the handwriting and I dropped it like it was covered with bugs.

"Where did you get that?" I asked.

"Lila brought it in a little while ago. She was down at McNeil's and Gerry gave it to her to return to you. He said he found it on the floor when he was cleaning up this morning."

I reached back in my mind to the day before and tried to make some sense out of this news. I knew I had put the letter in my pocket, but how did it get on the floor? Then I remembered putting my glasses in the same pocket when Troy came in, and realized that when I took them out I must have pulled the letter along with them. I looked down at my sandal and started to make circles on the rug.

"I repeat, when did you receive this?"

"Yesterday afternoon."

"And why didn't you tell us you heard from Jeff? You must certainly be aware of how concerned we are about him."

"Have you read the letter?"

"Of course not, it's addressed to you."

I knew a moment of relief, but it didn't last. I

knew they would respect my privacy, but I didn't know what to tell them was in the letter. They might be old, but they weren't dumb. They would realize Jeff had written to me because he didn't want them to know where he was and what he was up to. I thought of making up some story, but my imagination had suddenly gone dry on me. I did the only thing possible.

"Read it," I told them, feeling like a traitor.

Good for you, Hope, I thought as they pulled the letter out and started to scan it together. You've now managed to alienate every single person in the world you really care about.

Chapter 11
Mending fences

I was wrong. I hadn't managed to alienate everyone I cared about. There was still M. Lasseur, but I was able to complete my perfect record by Monday. It happened this way.

I went to class at nine-thirty as usual and, as usual, knocked on the door and walked in. I found M. Lasseur in his study, but instead of being behind his desk scowling at my latest homework assignment, he was standing beside a small table pouring wine into two glasses.

"Ah, Hope, my friend," he cried as I stood in the doorway staring. "Come in, come in." He held up the bottle for me to see. "We celebrate!"

I walked over to where he was holding out a glass of sparkling pale yellow liquid to me. Reaching out, I took the glass and said, "What is it?"

"Champagne, my dear. The only possible drink for such an occasion."

I'd never tasted champagne. I took a sip, still wondering what was going on, and immediately sneezed.

M. Lasseur laughed and said, "Ah, that often happens. The little bubbles go up the nose, yes?"

"Yes," I answered, feeling my face flush, and took another sip.

"What's the occasion?" I asked when I had recovered myself.

He beamed at me and reached into his pocket.

"I have heard at last from my wife," he exclaimed. "She and the boy are safe."

"That's wonderful news!" I cried. "Where are they?"

"She wrote from Sweden, but the letter is dated over a month ago. She hoped to be on her way over here before the autumn, but it is so difficult." For a moment the smile left his face, then he seemed to recover. "But that is of little importance beside the fact that she is out of France and the threat of the Nazi peril."

"Would they really have hurt her if she'd been captured?"

"Hurt her? Oh, my dear child. Do you not know what the Nazis are doing to the Jews in Europe? Had she and the boy been taken, I would

153

have prayed for quick death for them rather than the torture that would certainly have been their fate. God knows her life has been a nightmare as it is — working underground with the French Resistance, not having enough to eat, being in constant terror of capture."

It was hard for me to believe that such things were really going on. I'd heard of the prison camps where the Jews were sent, but I was pretty sure it was mostly a lot of propaganda to sell war bonds and get people to enlist and stuff like that. I didn't want M. Lasseur to think I doubted him though, so I tried to change the subject.

"How did she get out of France?"

"Some good friends who worked with her in the underground managed to smuggle her out. The Germans apparently were suspicious of the house where she and the boy were staying, and the rumour was that they were going to invade it. They escaped just in time." He gave an involuntary shudder and took a long drink from his glass. I began to feel quite uncomfortable. It was all so emotional and, well, foreign to me. I looked away from his tortured face and down at the letter he was clutching.

"Is that a picture in the envelope?" I asked as he began almost reverently to replace the letter.

"Ah, yes." His face brightened immediately. "That is my Stella and little Alex. Would you like to see it?"

I nodded, and he removed the picture and handed it to me as though he were presenting me with the crown jewels.

"Holy cow! This isn't the lady in the photograph. This is an old woman!"

I looked up in confusion. M. Lasseur's face had turned white. He snatched the picture out of my hand and turned away.

"I told you. She was with the French Resistance. It was not pleasant. It aged her a little, I suppose."

"I-I'm sorry. I didn't mean . . . " I stopped, not knowing what to say.

M. Lasseur turned back to me and put his glass down sharply on the table.

"Perhaps we will not have a lesson today." He took my half-empty glass from my hand and put it down beside his. "I will see you tomorrow." He turned and strode quickly out of the room.

I stood in the middle of the floor, contemplating the least painful way to rip out my tongue. I looked again at the photograph on M. Lasseur's desk of the beautiful woman holding the child and wanted to cry. The awful picture he had shown me today was printed on my brain. The poor woman. How could she stand having her beauty taken away from her like that? And M. Lasseur. How could he still love her when she looked so . . . I couldn't find words to describe the horrible change. Suddenly I needed to get away from that room and that picture and M. Lasseur. I ran out the door, down the hall and into the street.

I was still running when I got to Victoria Street. It was too early to go to work and too late to go home again. So I walked to the Commodore cafe and found myself a booth at the back where I could be alone for awhile.

I felt a little better after finishing off a forbidden chocolate malt, and decided to stroll slowly down to work, doing a little window-shopping on the way. Maybe Joyce's would have some panties with elastic — I was so sick of the buttoned variety we'd had to wear for the past four years. No panties, but a whole new shipment of cotton dresses. I forgot the time and spent the next hour trying on every size ten in the store.

By the time I got to McNeil's, the lunch crowd was just starting to gather. I rushed into the back and threw on my apron with Gerry's voice grumbling behind me.

I kept expecting Troy to come in any minute, but when my shift was finished at one-thirty and he still hadn't appeared, I gave up and went home. I was sure he would call sometime during the afternoon, but he didn't.

The house was empty. I went upstairs to try to memorize the vocabulary list M. Lasseur had given me days ago and to listen for the phone to ring. It was an aborted effort on both counts. By the time Mom came home at five-thirty, I was so lonesome I was ready to talk to the house plants. When I heard her come in the front door, I ran downstairs and threw my arms around her.

"Well, and to what do I owe this unexpected pleasure?" she asked, hugging me back.

"Nothing special. I guess I'm feeling a little down in the dumps."

"You and Lila still on the outs?"

"How did you know?"

"It was hard to miss, dear. Look, it's none of my business, but if I were you, I'd make up with her as soon as possible. She's a great girl, Hope."

"Yeah, I know. I'm going to do it when she comes home from work." But as it turned out, Lila went out for dinner, so I didn't get a chance to mend any fences until later that night.

She was lying on her bed reading when I

came in about eleven-thirty, and as I stood in the doorway wondering what to say, she put down her book and smiled at me. It was the first time since Saturday that she had noticed me.

"Ray called. He said you had phoned and apologized for Saturday night. That must have been hard to do, Hope."

Actually it hadn't been that bad. I didn't tell him about Troy; I just said I had a previous date that I'd forgotten about and didn't want to hurt his feelings, so I'd made up the story about being sick.

"I can understand why you've got this thing about Troy Farnham," Lila continued. "He's really good-looking. Any girl would go for him. But he's got a lot of problems. Believe me, I know. And don't get thinking I'm saying that because I want him for myself."

"I know that, Lila." I could feel my face turn red. "That was a stupid thing for me to say the other night and I'm so sorry. It's awful when we're fighting."

"I don't like it either, Hope. I'm sorry too for interfering, but it's only because I care a lot about you. Has Troy asked you out again?"

"No, and I don't suppose he will either." I

tried to sound unconcerned, but I was terribly afraid I might be right.

"Well, don't feel too badly about it." She looked rather relieved, I thought, maybe because that meant we wouldn't have to fight any more. "You're lucky to be free of him," she continued. "And you've got Ray, who's about a hundred times the man Troy is."

She might be right, but I knew that as long as my brain continued to function, I'd remember that evening at Tranquille. There was no point in trying to explain that to Lila though, so I changed the subject.

"Mom and Dad in bed?" I asked.

"Aunt Prue is. Your dad caught the bus for Vancouver a couple of hours ago."

"Oh, no. He's gone to get Jeff!"

"I expect so. Nobody has said anything to me, but I was the one who gave that letter to them. I didn't know at the time, of course, but I realize now it must have been from Jeff."

"It was," I groaned, and told her what he had written. "So now he'll think I betrayed him," I finished, bending my head so she wouldn't see the tears that were filling my eyes.

"I wouldn't worry too much, Hope. He should

never have asked you to help him that way. He put you in an awful position."

I looked up and saw her smiling at me. Without a word I went over to her bed and she put her arms around me.

"Poor little kid," she said. "It's been kind of a rough time for you, hasn't it?"

I nodded my head, thinking of M. Lasseur's anger, Anna and Shirley's coolness, and especially Troy's apparent lack of interest. "Boy, you don't know the half of it!"

"Never mind. Things will be better tomorrow."

* * *

But they weren't. I was sure glad Lila and I had made up, because the rest of that week was the living end and I could never have gotten through it on my own. M. Lasseur continued to be a frigid tyrant, both Shirley and Anna refused to talk to me, and Troy seemed to have disappeared from the face of the earth.

Then, just after the lunch crowd left on Friday afternoon, Troy came into the cafe.

"Hi," he smiled as he sat down at the counter. "Any chance of you whipping me up a root beer malted?"

160

I set about putting the shake together, aware that he was watching my every move and acutely conscious of my glasses. I didn't dare take them off and risk a repeat of the fiasco of last Saturday. I wanted to ask him why he hadn't called like he had promised, but I knew that would be about the dumbest thing I could do. So I took him his shake and waited for him to make the next move.

"About that date you promised me," he began as he reached for a straw. "Tonight okay?"

"But it's Friday, Troy. I have to work tonight."

"Aw, come on. You can miss one night, can't you?" He reached over and stroked my cheek. "I thought we might go out to Paul Lake."

Paul Lake! My thoughts raced back to the night of the party with the Takadas and how I had wished it was me instead of Laurie McVale who was with Troy at Paul Lake. Now was my chance, and I knew instinctively that I wouldn't have another. If I came on like a goody-two-shoes he would lose all interest in me. Before I could change my mind, I was nodding my head.

"I suppose I can skip work this once, Troy. I'll call in sick."

"Real fine. I'll pick you up about eight."

The last thing I wanted was for Lila to see

161

Troy picking me up. She was so dead against him. Now that we were friends again, I didn't want to do anything that would jeopardize our relationship. Besides, I was supposed to be at work, and how would I explain that one?

"No. I mean, don't come to the house. I'll meet you at the Anglican church on Nicola."

"Whatever you say. And, honey, please don't wear those glasses. They make you look like a college professor."

I blushed and pulled them off, but he was already up and walking toward the door.

There was only half an hour left of my shift, so I decided this would be the perfect time to set up my alibi. I got up, went behind the counter where Gerry was counting bills, and started to moan.

He looked up from the cash register and frowned.

"What's the matter with you?"

"I think I may have eaten something poisonous. My stomach is hurting something awful."

It probably wasn't the most diplomatic thing I could have come up with.

"Shhh! For Pete's sake don't let anyone hear you say that. You want to ruin my business?"

"I don't think it's anything I ate here, Gerry," I quickly recovered. "It was probably the raspberries I had for breakfast. The ice doesn't keep stuff like our old electric frig did."

He nodded absently and went back to his counting. "Maybe you'd better go home and take something for it. We're likely to have half the town in here tonight, and I'll need you."

I felt an awful twinge of guilt as I realized how I would be letting Gerry down. He'd need roller skates to stay even slightly behind if the crowds after the show were anything like last week. I really was starting to feel a little sick.

"I'll do my best," I promised, and went to the back to get my purse.

On my way home I saw Shirley heading toward me on the street. She must have been on her way back to the beauty parlor where she works. She didn't see me until we were almost in front of one another, and when she did notice me, she gave a start and tried to pass. I blocked her way.

"Look, I don't know why you're so mad at me, but if it's because of the weight I lost and stuff, I think you're being darned unfair."

She stopped and stared at me. Then, tucking her blouse into her too-tight shorts, she muttered, "It's not the weight you lost. I'm not that big a jerk. As a matter of fact, I'm on a diet myself. I've lost nearly five pounds."

"That's great," I answered.

"Well, you don't need to look so superior." She glared at me like she wanted to hit me, then the anger seemed to disappear and she spoke in a hurt voice. "Honestly, Hope, I didn't think you were the kind who would — Oh, never mind." She moved quickly to the side and tried to pass.

"No, don't go away." I grabbed her arm as she started to leave. "The kind who would what?"

"The kind who would bad-mouth her best friend just to make an impression on a boy," she said at last.

I looked blankly at her. "What are you talking about?"

"Don't pretend you don't know. Calling Anna the yellow peril and laughing when Troy Farnham talked about the enemy and polluting the air and all that garbage." Her face had turned red and she looked like she might explode all over the sidewalk.

"Oh, my gosh, Shirley. How do you know that?"

"Oh, come on, Hope! We were sitting right across from you. I guess I could have forgiven you if you hadn't known we were there — I would have figured you were trying to impress Troy or something dumb like that — but to deliberately insult one of your best friends is unforgivable."

I wanted to crawl under the nearest bush and not come out till school opened. No wonder neither she nor Anna would speak to me! I wouldn't have blamed them if they had stuck a burning cross on my front lawn.

I was desperately trying to think of something to say that would repair the damage, even a little bit, when Anna came up the street toward us.

"I thought I might catch you here, Shirl. Want to come over to the house for dinner tonight?" she said, completely ignoring me.

"Anna, please. I'm so sorry. I would never deliberately hurt you. You must know that."

She looked at me for a moment, then back at Shirley. "Do you know what she's talking about?"

"She wanted to know why we were ignoring her. I told her."

Then they both just stared at me.

I looked back at them pleadingly. "I didn't see you sitting across from us that night, I swear it. I didn't see anything. I wasn't wearing my glasses." I felt about two inches high, but I forced myself to say the words clearly.

As soon as she heard them, Anna started to laugh. She put her head back and roared for about five minutes. I just stood there watching her. If she wanted to laugh at me, she had certainly earned the right.

"Oh, Hope, you poor dumb nut," she sighed, wiping her eyes and smiling at me. "I suppose you weren't wearing your glasses so you could impress that Troy Farnham creep. You can't see your own shadow without your specs." The smile died away and pity filled her eyes. "Did looking good mean so much to you that you'd go around blind?"

I nodded miserably, then asked, "Could you possibly forgive me? Can we be friends again?"

"Yes, of course, Hope," Anna nodded. "Let's forget it ever happened."

"Super," I answered, but I knew I'd never forget what I had done if I lived to be fifty.

Shirley was still looking troubled though. "You still said those things, Hope, even though you didn't know we were there. Why?"

"You know I didn't mean them, Shirley. You were right, I was trying to impress Troy. I guess it was one of the dumbest things I've ever done in my entire life."

"That's for sure. Haven't you realized the

truth about Troy Farnham yet? Why don't you just forget about him, Hope? He's — "

Anna was nodding beside Shirley, but she must have noticed the expression growing on my face, because she suddenly broke in and saved the peace.

"Would you like to come over for dinner tonight too, Hope? We'll make it a kind of celebration."

What I wouldn't have given to be able to say yes. But it would mean cancelling my date with Troy, and that was just out of the question. Why did it seem like nothing could ever work out right?

"I'm sorry, Anna, I can't. I've got a date."

"A date? But don't you have to work tonight?"

"Uh, no. Gerry gave me the night off." When was I ever going to be able to stop lying?

"Okay, we'll make it another time. Have fun with Ray."

"I'm not — " I glanced at Shirley and broke off my explanation. "Yeah, thanks."

"We'll see you at the square dance tomorrow night anyway. Shirley and I are double dating. Do you and Ray want to join us?"

"I-I'll talk to you tomorrow. I've got to get

home now." I turned and ran till I couldn't see them behind me any more.

Why did I let Anna think I was going out with Ray instead of Troy? I wondered as I walked up the steps to the house. Was I ashamed of dating Troy? But that was absurd. He was the best-looking guy in Kamloops, and any girl would give her left elbow to go out with him. Wouldn't she?

Why was Shirley so down on him? Admittedly that scene she and Anna had heard at the Top Hat hadn't shown him in a good light, but he probably hadn't meant most of what he'd said that night anyway, just like I hadn't. Then, unbidden, the doubts I'd begun to have at the cafe returned to bother me. Was Troy really as great as he seemed, or could Lila and Shirley and Anna be right about him?

My head was starting to ache from so much thinking and I decided that all this soul-searching was just spoiling my mood. I had a date with Troy Farnham, and it was going to be the most exciting night of my life. Okay, so maybe some of my friends weren't happy about who I was dating, and maybe I'd had to tell a few fibs, but it was going to be worth it. A trip to Paul Lake!

By the time I got upstairs to my room, I'd shaken off the doubts and was as excited as I had been before I'd met Shirley and Anna.

Chapter 12
A fate worse than death

When I opened the door, I found Lila in our bedroom with every piece of clothing she owned lying all over the room. She was standing beside the bed in her bra and panties, looking like she had to decide the fate of the whole Italian army.

"Hi, how come you're home from work?" I asked from the doorway.

"Oh, Hope. Come in and help me decide. Do you think the blue cotton or the white rayon?" She held up two short-sleeved dresses with huge gathered skirts.

"For what? Where are you going?"

"Nowhere. I'm staying right here."

"Then why the big decision about what to wear?"

She gave me a smile that could light up London in a blackout.

"Johnny's home for the weekend. He's coming over at seven."

"Lila, that's terrific!"

"I guess maybe the white. It shows off my tan best, don't you think?" Without waiting for a reply, she wandered dreamily out the door toward the bathroom with the white dress across her arm.

For a moment I felt a rush of jealousy shoot through my chest. Johnny and Lila. The perfect couple. But so what? I had a date too. That was just as good or better. Wasn't it?

Ten minutes before eight, I slipped out of my room and tiptoed to the phone in the hall. I listened but could hear nothing. Johnny had arrived on the dot of seven, and he and Lila were out in the back garden. Mom had gone to play bridge with friends across town, and Dad was still in Vancouver. I gave the operator the number and waited for the ringing to be answered.

"Hello, Gerry? It's Hope. I'm awfully sorry, but I'm still pretty sick. I don't dare leave the house."

I could here him groaning at the other end of the phone.

"Geez, Hope, what a time to get sick! They're starting to come in already. Sure you can't make it?"

"I'm sure. I'll probably be okay tomorrow. I'm really sorry, Gerry."

"Yeah, I know you are. I'll try to get Cindy, but she usually won't work any night but Saturday. Well, take care of yourself and don't worry. I'll manage okay."

The sick feeling returned, and for a moment I was tempted to forget the whole plan and go to work as usual. Then I thought of Troy's hand on my cheek and my conscience took a nose-dive.

I went back to the bedroom, fixed my face and hair, and went downstairs. Lila was just coming in the back door as I reached the hall.

"You're leaving kind of early, aren't you, Hope? Why don't you come out back and have a lemonade with Johnny and me. He hasn't seen you since the big change."

"I can't, Lila. I promised Gerry I'd come in early tonight. He's expecting big crowds. And will you tell Mom I might be later than usual too?"

"Sure, Hope. But, gee, I'm sorry you have to work on a night like this. It would be a perfect time to go out to Ray's farm for a wiener roast and a swim."

I edged toward the door and muttered, "Well, that's the way it goes when you're a working girl. Have a good time and give my best to Johnny." I

172

ran out the door before she could delay me any longer. It was almost eight, and it was six long blocks to the church. I started to run down the hill. Troy might not stick around if I was late, I was afraid.

I got to the church on the dot of eight, but Troy hadn't arrived yet. I waited fifteen minutes and was just about to leave when I heard a car coming up the hill. It was going about forty miles an hour, with the horn honking. I just had time to take off my glasses and slip them into my purse before it screeched to a stop in front of the church and Troy's voice called out.

"Hi there, sweetie. Hop in."

I walked over to the car and opened the door. The smell of beer hung over the whole interior. For a fraction of a second I was tempted to close the door and walk away. Then Troy smiled at me, and I slid in beside him. He'd probably had only one or two, I convinced myself as I watched him skillfully manoeuver the car into a tight U-turn, then back to Battle Street and out the highway.

He didn't speak as we turned onto the road to the lake, and I began to feel nervous. I knew I ought to be coming up with scintillating conversational topics, but I had suddenly gone blank. I heard someone say once that you should talk about things that the man is interested in: sports, the war, cars. I decided to try sports.

"Do you play baseball, Troy?"

"Nope."

I tried again. "Do you listen to hockey on Saturday nights?" I was sure I was safe there. Everyone tunes their radio in to hockey on Saturday.

"Nope."

Maybe, I thought, I should move on to the war or cars. But before I could think of an intelligent comment to make, Troy spoke up on his own.

"Honey, would you mind cutting the chatter? I've got a head like you wouldn't believe."

"Oh, I'm so sorry. It's probably from the sun. A lot of people are getting sick with all this hot weather we've been having." I sounded like a character out of a comic strip.

He gave a rueful laugh. "No, it's not the sun."

Neither of us spoke for the next twelve miles.

I wondered what he had planned for us at the lake. Maybe we'd rent a boat and row up the lake in the moonlight like Johnny and Lila had done. There wasn't much else to do, since the lodge was out of bounds for anyone but the guests and there were no cafes or dance halls within miles. I settled back and thought of the next few hours.

*   *   *

"You look so lovely sitting there with the moon shining on your hair. I wish I could paint — I'd capture you for the whole of eternity."

"Oh, Troy, that's silly. You have so many girls to choose from. Why me?"

"No one is as beautiful as you, Hope. You're the only girl I ever want to be with."

"You mean you don't really like all those beautiful older girls?"

"No, I don't. You're all I want. Would you go steady with me? Here, I bought this locket for you."

"How beautiful! Oh, thank you!" I reached forward and kissed him on the cheek.

*   *   *

"Hey, don't you think we should wait till we get to the lake?"

I wanted to die. What if I'd said something out loud? But he wasn't laughing, so I assumed I hadn't disgraced myself that far.

I leaned back in my own seat and looked out the window. In a couple of minutes we came to the turnoff and approached the lodge and boat dock. Troy didn't slow down. We drove about half a mile along the lake, then turned onto another dirt road that led up the hill. It ended at a little cabin almost hidden by the tall pines that surrounded it. He stopped the car, reached into the back seat for a brown bag, and climbed out.

"Well, here we are," he announced, opening my door.

It was very dark and I couldn't see the path, but Troy took my arm and led me up the stairs and onto the porch.

The cabin was dark. There was no sign of anyone around the place. If there was a party going on, they must have run out of coal oil for the lamps, or else they were all sitting around in the dark. I wasn't sure I wanted to find out.

"Where are we?" I asked as I groped my way across the porch and stumbled against a chair.

"This is Aunt Jean's. She lets me use it whenever I want to get away from the maddening crowd."

"Is there a party going on?"

"Of course not. There's just the two of us. Isn't that the way you wanted it?"

My eyes were getting used to the dark and I could just make out a vague shape in front of me

176

that I assumed was Troy. The shape reached out a hand and pulled me down onto a wicker couch.

"There now, isn't that better?" He put one arm around me and reached into the paper bag with the other hand. He pulled out a bottle and released the cork with his teeth. I watched while he took a big swig, then he passed it over to me.

"No, thanks. I don't drink," I muttered in confusion.

"Come on. One little swallow won't hurt you. It'll loosen you up."

Before I could get control of myself, he had the bottle in my mouth and was tipping it up so the harsh wine poured down my throat and spilled onto my blouse.

He laughed and took another drink, then put the bottle down on the floor beside him and pulled me close. I leaned against his shoulder and pretended everything was going just great. Wine wasn't so bad. Maybe he was nervous and needed some liquid courage.

He turned to me and whispered, "Oh, Hope, this is going to be one spectacular night!"

His winy breath was on my face and he was searching for my mouth. He kissed me and it was heaven. I leaned toward him and put my arms around him. He kissed me again, only this time it

177

wasn't so gentle. His mouth was moving on mine and his tongue was trying to pry my lips open. At the same time, his right hand slid up from my waist and was on my breast, while his left started pulling my blouse out of my skirt band. This was *not* what I had planned. I tried to push him away, which only made him more aggressive. He was pulling at my clothes and his tongue was in my mouth. It was gruesome! I finally managed to get free of his hands and jumped to my feet.

"I'd like to go home, please."

He grabbed for me and pulled me back down on the couch.

"What the hell's got into you, Hope? This is what you wanted, isn't it?"

His mouth was on mine again, and his hands were back at their undressing act. I was scared to death. I thought of screaming, but there wasn't another cabin anywhere near. His whole body was pressing against me, and I felt like I was suffocating. Just when I was sure I was going to either throw up or faint, he eased away from me and reached down for the bottle. He took another long drink and I grabbed my opportunity, jumped up from the couch, and ran down the steps toward the car.

"Hey, where're you going?" His voice seemed to hold more surprise than anger.

I didn't answer as I threw open the door and slid under the wheel. I didn't have my license, of course, but I had a learner's permit and had been driving with Mom and Jeff for over a year. I knew I could drive the car home without any trouble. As I reached forward and felt for the keys, I heard Troy's footsteps pounding down the stairs.

"Come back here, you little tease!" he yelled. "I'm not through with you yet."

My hand shook as I groped around the dashboard. I had to get out of there before Troy reached the car and dragged me back into that awful place. Finally my blind fingers found the ignition, but the keys weren't in it.

I could hear Troy stumbling closer to the car. As quietly as I could, I slipped out the door and ran into the wooded area beside the road. Troy was still yelling for me to come back, and then he started demanding that I come out of hiding.

"I can see you, Hope. You might as well come out right now."

I dropped to my hands and knees and crawled behind a large bush. It was pitch black and I was pretty sure he was bluffing. I stayed hunched up and trembling behind the bush, ter-

179

rified that he might accidentally stumble over me as he thrashed about looking for me. Finally, after what seemed like about two years, he gave up and went back to the cabin. I heard the couch on the porch creak, and a minute later a bottle crashed on a rock somewhere in front of me.

I crawled back to the car and crept into the driver's seat again. I thought maybe the keys had fallen on the floor, so I bent over and began to feel around for them.

It was no use. Troy must have put them in his pocket when we stopped. I gave up hunting after about five minutes and leaned back against the seat. My only choice seemed to be to walk back toward town. With a little luck, I might even get a lift.

I stepped out of the car and started down the path to the lakeshore road. All around me the black night began to make strange sounds. I couldn't see a thing. I'd left my purse with my glasses in it on the porch when I made my escape. I didn't know if there were any wild animals this close to civilization, but I knew I didn't want to find out. I tried to remember how far we had travelled on the cutoff road to the cabin, and reckoned it must be about half a mile. The sounds got louder and more ominous. Before I had gone twenty paces, I knew I couldn't go through with it. Terror that was known beat terror that wasn't, I decided, and crept back to the car.

I knew Troy was furious with me, and his fury was something to reckon with. I was seeing a side of him that he'd kept very well hidden from me. I remembered Lila's warning and realized, a little late, I admit, that she probably was speaking from personal experience. No wonder she'd never dated him again! Why hadn't I listened to her and Shirley and Anna instead of getting angry and ignoring them?

What was I going to do now? I didn't know what Troy would do when he found me in the car, but I was sure it wouldn't be pleasant. But wait, maybe he wouldn't have to find me. If I could crouch down on the floor in the back seat, he might not see me. He would think I had walked back to the main road and was long gone. It was worth a try. I opened the back door and climbed in, praying that Troy didn't hear the creak it made when I pulled it shut. There was no sound from the porch, so after a minute of holding my breath, I pulled an old car rug that was lying on the seat over me and prepared to wait it out.

I lay there for what seemed like a long weekend, alternately shivering and crying. If only he would get bored and decide to go back to town. It was still early enough for him to find a more accommodating girl. In the end exhaustion must have taken over, because I finally fell asleep.

When I woke up, the car was moving. I had no idea where we were, and I was afraid to raise my head to peer out the side window. We seemed to be travelling about ninety miles an hour and weaving all over the road. Troy was singing at the top of his lungs and swearing between verses.

I was trying to figure out how I could slip away when we got to town, when the car suddenly veered to the right and went off the road. We bumped along for a few seconds, then came to a sudden stop. The jolt was tremendous, but I was fitted so tightly between the front and back seats that I barely moved.

I lay perfectly still, waiting to see what Troy would do. The motor was running, but he made no attempt to back the car up. After a moment, I realized there was no sound coming from the front seat. Slowly I raised my head and peered over the back rest. Troy was slumped over the wheel, blood all over his face.

I jumped out of the car and ran up to the road. There wasn't a car in sight. I had no idea where we were; it didn't look like the main road, but without my glasses I couldn't be sure. One thing I *was* sure of though — I had to get help.

I ran back to the car and opened the passenger door. I would have to pull Troy over from under the wheel if I was going to drive. The bleeding seemed to have stopped, and I could see that the cut on his forehead looked a lot worse than it really was. But his left leg was twisted at a very strange angle.

Somehow I managed to get him over into the passenger's seat without causing any more damage, and then climbed behind the wheel. I put the car in gear, and after three futile attempts, got it back on the road.

After a lot of searching, I found the knob that turned on the headlights and discovered they weren't working. I got out and went to the front of the car. The bumper was caved way in and both headlights were smashed. I'd have to drive blind, not that that would make much difference to what I'd see, but anyone coming toward me could easily plow right into me in the dark. Still, I had no choice.

I got back into the car and put it in first gear. After it had picked up speed, I shifted to second. We were going about twenty miles an hour and I couldn't see anything clearly past the windshield.

I left it in second and prayed nothing unexpected would loom up in front of me.

Nothing did for about five miles. Then, from out of the blue, or probably from over a hill, a car appeared. I was so startled I whipped the wheel to the right, and as the other car sailed past, I sailed into the ditch. Fortunately I didn't hit anything, and the car came to a quiet stop with its back wheels in the ditch and its front wheels in the loose dirt on the ridge above.

I was sure the other car would stop, but when I climbed out to flag it down, it had already disappeared over another hill. I went back to the car and looked it over. Nothing seemed to be broken, but when I got back behind the wheel and tried to start it, nothing happened.

Troy was still out cold, luckily. I was afraid his leg was broken, and much as I loathed him at the moment, I wouldn't wish that pain on anyone. I turned on the ceiling light and looked at my watch. I couldn't believe it was only ten-thirty. Ten-thirty on a Friday night, however, was not rush hour on the Paul Lake road. Everyone who was going out to the lake for the weekend would probably already be there, and certainly few people would be going back to town. I began to panic again.

184

I knew I had to get help for Troy very soon. The cut on his forehead didn't look serious, but I had no way of knowing whether he might have something wrong inside. Old episodes of "Calling Dr. Kildare" ran through my head, and within minutes I had Troy suffering from concussion, punctured lungs, crushed liver and internal bleeding. There was no getting around it this time — I would simply have to walk back to town.

Setting out down the highway wasn't quite as bad as it had been earlier when I tried to walk back to the lakeshore road. The moon had come out and I could almost see my feet. Besides, we had stopped at the edge of the forested area, and on either side were wide open fields. It was still terribly scary though, and my crazy imagination conjured up wild dogs and crazed killers at every turn in the road.

I would have given anything for a pair of my glasses, even the black-rimmed ones. Everything was so blurred and unfamiliar. I could follow the road, of course, but I felt like I was walking on the moon. I would also gladly have traded my left toe for a pair of saddle shoes, preferably old ones. I was wearing new sandals with wedge heels that kept catching on stones in the road and rolling me over on my ankles. The straps were cutting into the back of my heels, and the old blisters I had got on my first day of work were making another guest appearance. I was a mess, and I was tired, and I was scared.

I trudged along for half an hour without meeting or being passed by a car. It looked like I was going to have to walk the whole way to town, which might take me hours. I wasn't even sure whether I was on the main road. In fact, I wasn't even sure I was going in the right direction. I had no way of knowing where Troy was headed before we crashed. Maybe I'd be wandering around in the wilderness on some deserted side road for the rest of my probably short life. And Troy would wake up with a broken leg and crushed insides and die of neglect on the front seat of his Ford. I was crying so hard that when the car came up behind me, I didn't hear it.

Chapter 13
Rescued

"There she is!"

"Pull over, quick!"

"She's limping. She must have been in an accident!"

I looked up and saw through the blur of my tears and my myopia that a car had drawn up on the other side of the road and a bunch of people were pouring out. I had no idea who they were until I heard the unmistakable voice of my brother.

"Hopeless, oh, my God! Are you okay?"

Four bodies loomed up in front of me, and I was surrounded by Lila, Johnny, Jeff and Ray. Ray was the first to reach me and, blubbering like a five-year-old, I threw myself into his arms.

Everyone was talking at once.

"What happened?"

"Where's Troy?"

"What are you doing way out here?"

"Are you hurt?"

"I'm okay now," I sniffed, moving away from Ray and trying to smile. "Boy, am I glad to see you guys!" Suddenly it hit me. I was seeing Jeff; I must be hallucinating again. I reached out and touched him.

"Jeff, are you really real?"

"Of course I'm real. But you don't seem to be. What happened?" he repeated. "And where's Troy? You *were* with him, weren't you?"

"Troy! Oh, Lord! He's back there in the car. I think his leg's broken, and I don't know what else. We have to get him to the hospital right away."

I limped across the road and opened the passenger door of Ray's car. "Hurry, please," I called as I climbed in. Ray was behind the wheel in seconds, and the others weren't far behind.

"Where's the car, Hope?" he asked. "We didn't see it on the way down here."

"It's in a ditch just past where the forest starts. I guess it must be kind of hidden by the trees."

We found the car a couple of minutes later. Troy was sitting on the back fender drinking a bottle of wine. He started yelling at us as we drove up.

188

When we got out and went over to him, I could see that his leg was still at that funny angle and his face was contorted in pain.

"God! I didn't think anyone was ever going to come along." Then, seeing me, he gave a sickly grin. "So you were the one to bring the rescue squad, eh? How did you know where to find me?"

"I was the one who drove the car into the ditch," I answered matter-of-factly.

I hadn't had a chance to tell the others what had happened, and they all stared at me like I had just grown another arm.

"You broke my leg? Oh, baby, you really know how to get revenge, don't you?"

"You broke your own leg when you drove the car into a tree about five miles back there. If you check the front bumper and the headlights, you'll see where they were hit, and it sure wasn't in this ditch." I was so angry with him I could hardly speak.

"You drove the car, Hopeless? With no glasses and no headlights?" Jeff sounded incredulous.

"I didn't have much choice," I retorted. "This drunken idiot was out cold."

Lila, who had not spoken nor let go of my hand since we got out of the car, finally spat out,

"You ought to be locked up, Troy Farnham. You could have killed yourself — not that that would have been much of a loss — but you could have killed Hope too, and that would have been."

"Look, I'm sorry. I guess I screwed up royally, but right now my leg's on fire. I need to get to a doctor."

The boys half carried him to the car and got him into the front seat. The rest of us piled on top of each other in the back. In fifteen minutes we were in the emergency room of the Royal Inland Hospital.

The intern there insisted on checking me out as well, but all he found were the blisters. Troy was taken up to surgery, and the rest of us left the hospital and drove to our house.

Mom and Dad were both home when we got there. They knew nothing about what had happened, and I was dreading having them find out. Lila and Jeff, however, didn't seem to think it was necessary to burden them with the truth. As soon as we got there, Lila slipped up to our room and brought down my extra glasses before anyone noticed them missing. And when Mom asked where we'd been, Jeff calmly answered, "Oh, we all just went for a little drive."

"That's nice, dear," Mom answered. "Isn't it wonderful to have Jeff home?"

I looked over at my brother. We had been too busy and too preoccupied for him to say much of anything to me since they found me on the road. But we weren't too busy now, and I waited for the explosion. Instead, he grinned at me.

"Don't look so stricken, Hopeless. I don't blame you for showing the letter to the folks. In fact," he glanced sheepishly at Dad, "I'm kinda glad you did. I guess I really wanted to come home when I found out that the guy who was going to forge my birth certificate got caught and I could have been sent up too if I'd gone along with him."

Dad came over and patted him on the shoulder. "It's good to have you home, son." He rubbed his hand across his eyes and grabbed Mom's hand. "Come on to bed and leave these young people alone."

Mom grinned and followed him out the door.

When we were alone, the questions finally came. I told them everything that had happened, and when I got to the part on the porch, I was afraid Jeff was going to storm back to the hospital and break Troy's other leg.

"Look, it's not entirely Troy's fault," I said. "He didn't exactly force me to go with him."

"But you're only a kid, Hope," Johnny protested. "He had no right to do that to you."

"He sure as hell didn't!" Jeff agreed.

"No, I asked for everything I got. I was warned enough times and just wouldn't listen. What I don't understand is how you knew where to find me."

"It wasn't hard," Lila answered. "When your dad and Jeff came home — a friend of your dad's flew them back — Jeff phoned Ray right away. Ray drove right over here and we all piled into his car and went looking for you at McNeil's. Of course, when we found out you hadn't been in, Jeff went crazy."

"Gerry said you'd phoned in sick," Jeff continued. "We knew then there was something funny going on."

"Then Anna and her boyfriend came in. We asked her if she knew where you were, and she told us you had a date. She had just assumed it was with Ray, she said. That was when we knew you had to be with Troy."

"It wasn't hard to figure out where you'd be. We all know about Troy's little hideaway at the lake where he takes his girls," Johnny explained, "so we were pretty sure where to look for you. We were afraid he would try to pull something."

"But how come you didn't pass us when you were going up? You would have recognized Troy's car, wouldn't you?"

"You weren't on the main road, Hope," Jeff said. "You were on that old road that parallels it. When we found the cabin deserted and fresh butts in the ashtray, we figured you had to be on the old road."

"No wonder there was hardly any traffic," I exclaimed. The realization of what could have happened suddenly hit me and I started to shake. "I could have wandered around on that road for days before anyone found me," I cried.

"Maybe, but you didn't. You're home safe now. So why don't you go on up and hit the sack? You've had quite a night." Jeff came over and kissed my cheek. "You may be hopeless, but you're the only sister I've got."

"I'll come with you," Lila said as she stood up. Then to Johnny, "I'll see you tomorrow — early, okay?"

Johnny nodded and smiled at her like he wanted to eat her up.

I looked over at Ray. He hadn't said much since I had thrown myself in his arms out on the abandoned road. I wondered if he would ever forgive me for all my lies and deceit. I tried to smile, but it didn't quite come off.

"I'll see you around, Hope," he said as he stood up to leave. "I'm glad you're okay."

"Thanks," I replied, waiting for him to make the next move. But he just smiled again and walked out the door.

When we got upstairs, I threw myself on the bed and started to cry.

"That's not going to do much good, Hope," Lila said.

"It's the aftermath of shock," I answered, dredging up the expression from my grade B movie vocabulary.

"No, it's not. You got over that a long time ago. You're crying because of Ray."

I began to protest, then realized she was quite right.

"We were supposed to go to the barn dance together tomorrow night," I blubbered. "But he didn't even mention it. I guess he doesn't want to have anything more to do with me, and I don't blame him."

"Maybe, but I don't think so. Why don't you call him tomorrow and just ask him?"

"Oh, I couldn't do that!"

"Of course you could. And you have to. Remember, Hope, you made it pretty clear that you preferred Troy Farnham to him. He probably thinks you don't have much use for him."

"But that's not true! It's just that he doesn't make me feel . . . well, you know."

"Give it a chance. You've been so blinded by Troy Farnham's looks that you lost all perspective."

I didn't say anything for a minute or two. Maybe she was right. It wouldn't be the first time. "Okay, I'll call him first thing in the morning. But I wouldn't blame him if he slammed the phone down in my ear."

"He won't. Now go wash your face and come to bed. You want to look good tomorrow, don't you?"

After what I'd been through, I wasn't sure I did.

*   *   *

I woke up early the next morning and rolled over on my side to gaze out the window. Not a cloud in the sky. It would probably be hot in the afternoon, but it would be perfect for the barn dance in the evening.

Everyone would be going: Lila and Johnny,

Anna and Billy, Shirley and Lyle. I supposed I could go stag if Ray wouldn't take me, and it didn't look to me like he would. But how would I get there? Of course, I could always ask Jeff to take me. Wouldn't that look great — arriving at the biggest party of the summer with my brother! I was a whole lot better off when I was fat and spotty.

*   *   *

"Hey, Hope, meet you at the corner at one-thirty. It's a perfect swimming day."

"Okay, Shirl," I answered. "But I want to be home early to get ready for the barn dance tonight."

"You and Ray are coming with us, aren't you?"

"We sure are. I still don't know what he sees in me," I laughed. "I'm overweight and near-sighted and pimply."

"Maybe, but you've got a great personality, Hope. And you're a good friend. People can depend on you to do the right thing."

"Thanks, Shirley, but ... "

*   *   *

"Great Swith! I'm starting to fantasize myself fat

and ugly again!" I muttered. What was happening to me anyway?

I rolled out of bed and slumped down to the bathroom. Lila was still sleeping like the dead. Easy for her, she had absolutely nothing to worry about. I thought about our conversation the night before and resolved that as soon as I had breakfast, I'd phone Ray.

I grabbed a bottle of shampoo, stepped into the tub and turned on the shower. I didn't even bother to look in the mirror; I'd probably lost another pound or two and I didn't want to know about it.

When I climbed out of the tub, I wrapped myself in an old terry towel robe and went downstairs. Mom was the only one in the kitchen. She was drinking coffee and reading the *Kamloops Sentinel*, our eight-page daily paper.

"It says here that Troy Farnham is in the hospital with a broken leg. Isn't that the boy you went for a drive with the other night, Hope?" she asked.

I dropped to a chair in mild shock. What if the paper mentioned me? Mom would never trust me again, and I wouldn't blame her.

"It says he was brought into the hospital after he was found in his wrecked car by a group

197

of friends. He was all alone out on the old lake road. My, my, how strange." She shook her head and turned the page. I started breathing again. "I'm certainly glad you weren't with him, Hope. I'd have been worried sick."

I started to smile to myself. Saved again, I thought. Then I began to realize that the pattern was repeating itself. They say if you do something three times it becomes a habit. This would be my third major lie, and I didn't like the feeling.

"Mom, I've got to tell you something."

"Yes, dear?" She continued to scan the paper.

"Please, put the paper down and listen to me. I *was* with Troy Farnham last night. I phoned in to work sick and drove out to the lake with him. He started drinking and got, well, overly friendly." She didn't say a word as I recounted everything that had happened the night before. "And now Ray doesn't like me anymore," I finished. "I guess that's my punishment, unless you had something in mind yourself?"

"Oh, Hope. My poor darling little idiot. What a thing to have gone through! No, I'm not going to punish you. You've been punished enough. And I suspect I'll never have to worry about you ever pulling anything like that again."

"Don't worry! I'm so sick of lies and deceit. And I'm sick of being pretty too. All it's got me is trouble."

She raised her eyebrows and said, "Oh, really?"

"That's for sure." She didn't argue the point, so I went on. "Do you think I should call Ray? Lila says it's the right thing to do."

"I agree with Lila. Go do it now before you lose your nerve."

I got up and went slowly to the phone.

"Ray, it's me. Hope."

"Yes, I know."

"I just phoned to thank you for finding me last night."

"That's okay. But it was Johnny who really knew where to look."

It wasn't exactly going like I'd hoped. He didn't sound a bit friendly. But then, why should he? I decided that he really did deserve an explanation, and a better one than I'd given him before.

"Ray, I'm so sorry about the way I've been lately. Last Saturday I didn't have another date; I went out with Troy."

"I know."

"You know? How could you?"

"Troy told me. He couldn't wait to brag about taking my girl away from me."

"Your girl?"

"Well, sure. At least I hoped that was what you were. But I guess I was wrong. How could I expect you to look twice at me now that half the male population of Kamloops wants to date you?"

"That's not true."

"Sure it is. Look, Hope, I've gotta go. Dad needs me to help him with some thinning in the orchard. I'll be seeing you."

The phone went dead. So much for Lila's predictions. My heart had started thumping for a minute, but it was obvious that Ray had no intention of taking me to the dance.

Lila came down the stairs just as I was getting up from the hall table. I guess I looked like I'd been given twenty years in the salt mines because she came right over and put her arm around me.

"What happened, Hope? Did you call Ray?"

"Yes, and I confessed about last Saturday night. But he already knew."

"I thought you said you told him about that last Sunday?"

"I didn't tell him the real truth. It was just another of my famous lies."

"I see. Did he mention the barn dance?"

"Not a word."

"Never mind. You can come with Johnny and me. I bet Ray hasn't got a date, and when you see him face to face you can make up."

"Oh, Lila! I can't go with you and Johnny. That would be even worse than going with Jeff!"

"Then I'll tell Johnny I'll meet him there and we'll go together."

"Would you do that for me?"

"Of course. Johnny won't mind. Naturally I'll come home with him," she grinned, "since you'll be with Ray."

I watched her as she glided into the kitchen looking like a ballerina. I'd wanted so much to be like her — pretty and popular — and now I was. But I wasn't really like her at all. Lila would never lie or be deceitful or hurt people the way I had done. I wanted to blame my ugly behaviour on my change in appearance, but that just didn't wash. Pretty and nice didn't have to be opposites — Lila proved that. I had a lot more apologizing to do if I was going to be able to look in the mirror again. And I knew where I would start.

Chapter 14
More fences

M. Lasseur didn't answer my knock right away. I thought of letting myself in as I usually did, but decided against it. This wasn't a lesson day so he wouldn't be expecting me. When he did come to the door, he was wearing an apron over his dressing gown. He looked startled when he saw me standing on the porch.

"It is you, Hope. So dedicated to your studies that you come on a Saturday?"

"No, I came to talk to you. May I come in?"

He looked at me for a moment before moving aside and gesturing me to enter. Without a word, he walked down the hall to the kitchen. Wishing I were somewhere else, preferably at the other end of the country, I followed.

"I am making myself French toast — very Canadian." A little smile crossed his lips. "May I offer you a slice?"

I realized that I hadn't had any breakfast,

and the smells coming from the stove were making me drool, but I didn't want to push my luck.

"No, thank you, but you go ahead." As I shook my head, my stomach howled like a wounded puppy.

His smile got bigger. He lifted a plate down from the cupboard and slipped two slices of toast and three strips of bacon on it, then handed it to me.

"If we are to have a serious talk — and it would appear that is what you have in mind — we must first appease our hunger."

He sat down across from me and began to eat. Judging that this was not the time to begin expressing my repentance, I picked up my knife and fork and followed suit. We ate in complete silence.

When he had finished, M. Lasseur wiped his mouth with his napkin, drained the last of his coffee, and said, "Very well. Let us hear what you have to say that is so important it makes you come here on such a beautiful day."

"It's about last Monday. I owe you an apology."

"True."

I waited, but he didn't say anything more; he just sat looking at me expectantly.

"I didn't mean to be rude, but when you showed me your wife's picture, I guess I was . . . well, shocked. She was so beautiful, and now . . . " I was succeeding admirably in talking myself into a very tight corner. "What I mean is . . . "

M. Lasseur nodded soberly. "I know what you mean, Hope. I should not have been so angry with you. You are very young, and to the young, physical beauty is everything."

I began to play with my spoon, feeling like some sort of mental freak.

"But when one becomes older, one sees beauty in a different light. My Stella was a very beautiful woman; I was the envy of all our friends when she consented to be my wife. That was the Stella you see in the photograph on the desk. But the Stella you saw in the picture that shocked you is to me even more beautiful. Where there was once smooth skin, there are now lines of character that she has earned through pain and toil and fear. Those lines are more precious to me than the most flawless complexion of the most glamorous cinema star. Do you comprehend at all what I say?"

"I would very much like to see the picture again," I replied.

He hesitated for a moment, then reached into his pocket and handed me the small snapshot. I looked at it and tried to see what he saw. At first I saw only the tired face with its premature wrinkles and sad eyes. Then the eyes seemed to lose their sadness and I could see in them a wise smile. My gaze travelled down to the firm mouth with its full lips and the strong determined chin under it. The wrinkled cheeks and lined forehead began to fade. The woman in the picture I held in my hand *was* truly beautiful. How could I possibly not have seen it before?

I smiled and handed back the picture. "I see what you mean. I really do," I said quietly.

He took the picture and held it like he was holding the Hope diamond. He gazed at me for a long time without speaking. Then he said, "Yes, I think you do," and smiled widely.

He jumped up from the table and rubbed his hands. "More coffee?" he asked, but before I could reply, he shook his head and said, "No, no. Not coffee," and went over to the icebox. He reached in and pulled out the bottle of champagne he had opened last Monday.

"Perhaps it has lost a bit of its fizz, but we

will pretend." He took down two glasses, filled them to the brim and handed one to me. "Now we celebrate. A toast."

"No, let me," I insisted. "To your beautiful wife and son. May you all be together very, very soon." My eyes were filled with tears, so I couldn't see M. Lasseur's face. I hoped he wouldn't think I was being a forward brat.

I guess he didn't, because he said, "Now my turn. To my beautiful new friend, Hope. May all her lines be laugh lines."

We both tipped our glasses back and drained them. And I didn't sneeze.

When I finally left M. Lasseur's house, I didn't go home. Instead, I climbed the hill south of the town to Bridalveil Falls. I needed to be alone for awhile. There was this girl, Hope Mather, I used to know, and I figured it was time we got reacquainted.

Bridalveil Falls is only a short distance from our house, but going there is like being in another country. It's been left completely un-touched, and except for the remains of old camp-fires, it looks like it's never seen a human being. I used to go there a lot when I was younger. Anna and Shirley and I would load up with a quarter's worth of wieners and buns and half a dozen Pepsi and stay for the day. It was my favourite place on earth.

I arrived at our secret spot behind the second falls in about fifteen minutes. I hadn't seen anyone on my way in; too hot for most people, I guessed. Seating myself with my back against a big rock, I thought about the past week.

Mom was right, as usual. It wasn't the change in my looks that had got me in trouble, it was the way I was handling the change. Suddenly I was living one of my fantasies and I didn't know how to cope with it. A person's daydreams should never come true, I decided. It just wasn't healthy. In less than two weeks I had changed from a decent, friendly, honest girl to a conceited little liar. No wonder Lila said she liked me better when I was fat and ugly.

But wait a minute. Did I have to be that different? I had learned a few things from Troy and M. Lasseur over the last couple of days, not least of which was how little the outside packaging really meant. The girl who Ray thought was pretty when she looked like a pregnant sow was still the same person underneath. She could be that girl again, only without a spare tire and acne. But it wasn't going to happen all by itself. I would have to make all the moves first; after all, I was the one who had messed up.

I sat looking at the water tumbling over the big rocks in front of me and planned what I would do. At last, when the sun had moved behind the pine trees, I got up and went home.

"Lila, can I talk to you for a minute?"

She was sitting at the dressing table combing her wet hair. When I had come in, I had seen that the table was set for dinner. We would be eating momentarily, but I had to apologize to Lila first.

"Sure, Hope, what's the problem?"

"I've done a lot of dumb things in the past week, but one of the dumbest was to lose your respect. I just want you to know that I think you're the greatest thing since technicolour, and I want to be just like you when and if I ever grow up."

She caught my eye in the mirror and gave me a skeptical look. Then I guess she must have realized I was dead serious. She put down the comb and turned around on the bench.

"Don't want to be like me, Hope. Want to be like yourself. You're a terrific person when you're not trying to be someone else."

"Not as terrific as you," I grinned. "But then

208

maybe when I'm as old as you, I'll have caught on to the secret."

Mom called us for dinner just as she took aim at me with a large pillow.

When we were all sitting at the table, I brought up the subject of the barn dance again.

"About tonight, Lila — tell Johnny you'll drive out with him. I'll find my own way."

"You certainly won't. At least you'll come with us."

I hesitated for just a moment, thinking about my stupid image. Then reality started to rear its sensible head and I said, "Are you sure you don't mind? I could sit in the back and be practically invisible."

"I don't see why you should do that, Hopeless, when I've got an empty front seat."

"You'd take me? Your baby sister?"

"Why, ma'am, I'd be mighty proud," Jeff answered, trying to sound like Rhett Butler. "Unless, of course," he continued in his normal voice, "you'd be embarrassed going with your brother."

"Why, sir," I retorted in an even worse southern accent, "y'all are just so kind. I surely would be mighty proud too."

And I was.

*   *   *

The place was packed when we got there. I had
wanted to wear my old jeans and shirt, but Lila
had practically forced me into a bright red square
dance dress and white ballerinas.

"Don't be silly about your looks, Hope. Just
because you make the most of yourself doesn't
mean you're conceited, you know."

I supposed she was right, and it *was* fun
being popular, but I wore my glasses just the
same.

Jeff and I split up as soon as we arrived, and
I searched through the crowd on my own. I
spotted Anna and Shirley and their dates as they
joined a new square that was forming, but I just
waved to them and moved on.

I finally found Ray in the middle of the floor
with another of the squares, and watched from
the sidelines as the four couples do-si-doed and a-
la-mained-left to the voice of the caller. I wondered which of the girls he was with and if he had
brought her to the dance.

When the set was over, he bowed to a pretty
little redhead who was in the grade behind me,
and I felt my stomach do a fast a-la-main-left of
its own. Then he left the girl and walked over to

210

sit down a few yards away. I was pretty sure he had seen me standing against the wall, but he certainly paid no attention. It was up to me.

The band had gone into a slow waltz and the lights were turned way down low. I took a deep breath, pushed my glasses up on my nose, and walked over to him.

"It's not Ladies' Choice, but will you dance with me anyway?"

I couldn't tell if he was pleased or just surprised.

"Okay," he answered, a bit reluctantly. He stood up and reached out his right hand to take mine.

I ignored the outstretched hand and took his left instead, deliberately wrapping my fingers around the stump.

He gave a quick jerk of surprise and stared intently at my face for a moment, then squeezed my hand and led me onto the dance floor.

"The gang is going to Fish Lake tomorrow to see how the trout are biting," he announced as he put his arms around me. "Want to come along?"

"I can't think of anything I'd rather do," I answered with the biggest smile of my life. "Unless, of course, it would be to sit in the living room and watch 'Fibber McGee and Molly' on a magic box."

"You still don't believe me about television, do you?"

"Oh, Ray, how could anybody believe such nonsense?" I chided him. "It's like telling me that someday a man will walk on the moon."